S. G. WILSON

Illustrations by Aleksei Bitskoff

Random House 🏠 New York

Visit us on the Web! rhcbooks.com

Educators and librarians, for a variety of teaching tools, visit us at
RHTeachersLibrarians.com

Library of Congress Cataloging-in-Publication Data
Names: Wilson, S. G., author. | Bitskoff, Aleksei, illustrator.
Title: Pleased to meet me / S. G. Wilson; illustrations by Aleksei Bitskoff.
Description: New York: Random House, 2020. | Series: Me vs. the multiverse; 1
Summary: "Thirteen-year-old Meade Macon attends Me Con, a convention
where he meets different versions of himself from across the multiverse"—
Provided by publisher.
Identifiers: LCCN 2019037880 (print) | LCCN 2019037881 (ebook) |
ISBN 978-1-9848-9575-2 (hardcover) | ISBN 978-1-9848-9576-9 (lib. bdg.) |
ISBN 978-1-9848-9577-6 (ebook)
Subjects: CYAC: Identity—Fiction. | Multiverse—Fiction. | Congresses and
conventions—Fiction. | Science fiction.
Classification: LCC PZ7.1.W578 Pl 2020 (print) | LCC PZ7.1.W578 (ebook) |
DDC [E]—dc23

Printed in the United States of America
10 9 8 7 6 5 4 3 2 1
First Edition

For
E., W., and O.

★ ★ ★

Contents

The Origami Stalker

So this one time when I was six, I went sleepwalking and peed in my tub of Legos. I never told a soul, and no one in the world could have possibly known. But seven years later, the ugly truth was right there, scrawled on a note inside an origami octopus. I found it first thing in the morning hanging by its arms from the sill of my bedroom window:

Hi, Me,

Yes, you. You're me, and I'm you.
    Don't believe me? Here's proof. This is stuff only we would know:

  1. After peeing in our Lego container while sleepwalking when we were six, we dumped

the pieces in the dishwasher. Lego Yoda's lightsaber broke the dishwasher pump, and we got in serious trouble.

2. Since age three, we've had a recurring nightmare about an otter forcing us to do push-ups and climb ropes in army boot camp.

3. We'd never fess up to anyone that greeting card commercials, pet-adoption pop-up stands, and the friendship pictures on Girl Scout cookie boxes always make us a little weepy. So do most Pixar movies. Except maybe Planes.

Anyway, learn more about what we have in common by coming to the Janus Hotel South anytime today. I'll explain more soon.

Ours sincerely,
Me

Though I'd never seen this note before in my life, it was written in my handwriting. Not the "neat" writing I attempted for teachers, but the unreadable scrawl I used the rest of the time.

It only got weirder from there. Whoever had made the octopus used a special fold I'd invented and thought nobody else knew how to do. I'd dreamed it up from the picture of a real-life Atlantic pygmy octopus I saw in one of Dad's *National Geographics*, where I got most of my origami ideas. I must have made it hundreds of times, but I'd only ever shown my best friend, Twig, how to do the folds. Smart as she was, she'd never gotten the hang of it.

If she hadn't folded it, who had?

I looked out the window and saw no sign of anybody. Maybe this was Twig's idea of a joke. She could have swiped one of my old octopus folds and mimicked my writing easily enough. But that just didn't seem like something she'd do. Besides, how would she have known my deepest, darkest secrets? I'd told her a lot about myself, but I'd stayed mum on the Legos and the pee. And the greeting card commercials, for that matter.

Then there was the Janus Hotel. Why would anybody want to meet at an abandoned building like that? I was pretty sure my parents had met for the first time at some conference there way back when, but the place had been out of business for a few years now.

I reread the note a half dozen times as I got ready for school and headed downstairs to breakfast. It was one of those mornings when Mom sat at the table and Dad stood at the counter so they didn't have to talk to each other. That was how they fought—arguing without actually saying anything.

When I walked in, they strapped weak smiles on their faces. They weren't very good actors. Before either of them could start in with the public service announcements ("Use a fork, not your fingers," "Chew with your lips closed," "Fart in private, not at the table"), I asked a question: "Didn't you used to go to some conference at the old Janus Hotel?"

Dad's face turned dreamy. He always got this way when he remembered the early days of Me Co., the fitness-watch company he'd started before I was born. "Why, yes, Meade, I had a lot of great conferences there."

"Ahem," said Mom. She actually said "ahem" instead of just clearing her throat. "It's also where we met."

Dad's smile faded and he straightened up. "Right, of course." Then the smile crept back. "Your mom was at a physics conference going on in the hotel at the same time as mine. The two conferences double-booked the ballroom for a party, but nobody minded and we all mingled. I didn't go in for parties much, so I was off in the corner trying to fix a busted processor. Then I heard a voice say—"

"'Excuse me, do you know anything about laptops?'" Mom recalled. She smiled too. "I had motherboard issues."

For just a minute, the ice between them melted and they gazed at each other in a really embarrassing way. Two nerds in love. Then they seemed to remember they were mad and got back to sulking.

"Right," I said. "I've heard that story before." Like a zillion times.

"Why do you ask?" said Dad.

"Just curious." Could the note writer have possibly known that my parents met at the Janus, or was that reading too much into this? All I knew was that I could never

4

show them the octopus. I didn't need them thinking I'd been writing stalker notes to myself. They were already on my case enough as it was.

I polished off my breakfast in the fewest bites possible and headed for the door. That's when the MeMinder ratted me out. "Reminder!" said the watch in its stupid robot voice. "Full dress rehearsal at drama class. Basketball practice after school. Science fair project only one percent complete. Must complete science fair project for Student Showcase Night tonight!"

Me Co. made one product, the MeMinder, and I wore the latest version on my wrist. I couldn't have told you if it was the MeMinder 8 or the MeMinder 9. As the company's lone product tester/guinea pig, I'd started losing count after the MeMinder 4. It had been bad enough when earlier MeMinders tracked my exercise and sleep, but this new model made things even more torturous by keeping tabs on "personal goals."

"Is that thing glitchy, or are you really that far behind on your project?" Mom asked.

As former science fair winners themselves, Mom and Dad were a little too keen on me placing in the contest. I wanted to place too, if only to get them off my back. Plus, I figured they might not fight with each other so much if they had a son who'd actually accomplished something. The only problem was, I stank at science like I stank at every-thing else, and no idea for a project had come to me. It was like my brain had locked up from the pressure. Now I'd have to scramble after school to get something together. Worse came to worst, I could mount some origami on a poster and call it geometry. But I'd wanted to do so much more.

"Nah, it's all done."

"Lie detected," said the MeMinder. "Achieve-O-Meter shows one percent completed on project."

"When did this thing get so smart?!" I said.

"It works!" Dad did a dorky dance but stopped when Mom glared at him. "Never mind that. You need to get moving on your project. It's a big goal."

Mom and Dad always talked a good game about achieving goals, but it's not like they spoke from experience. Mom was still only an assistant professor, and Dad had to work a day job at a tech company that actually made money, since Me Co. didn't. So who were they to harp on me about achieving stuff?

Before they could harass me more, I grunted a goodbye and headed out the door.

Where I found another origami waiting for me on the doorstep.

★ 2 ★

Origam-Me

It had taken me weeks to perfect the origami honey badger, my second-favorite creation after the origami octopus. I'd felt proud knowing that this, like the octopus, was a unique fold that nobody could duplicate unless I showed them how. That's why it wasn't just scary to see one of my honey badgers sitting there outside my house; it was infuriating. Either somebody was stealing my origami, or my origami weren't so unique after all.

I nearly unscrewed my head from my neck looking around for whoever had left the new note. No sign of anybody. My hands shook as I picked up the honey badger, unfolded it, and read a note inside. Just like the first, it was written in my handwriting, but with words I had never put to paper.

Hi, Me,

Making the schlep to school on a bike again? Lots
of Mes across the multiverse own an electric
scooter. Learn how you can get one too by coming
to the old Janus Hotel South after school.

Ours sincerely,
Me

Multiverse? Now, there was something that finally made
sense. Mom had studied the theory of parallel dimensions
for her PhD work in physics. She'd even done experiments
back in the day to prove that alternate Earths existed. The
experiments had failed, and nobody wanted to publish her
ideas, but she'd never stopped loving the subject. She'd still
go on and on about the science behind mirror realities whenever they came up in TV shows and movies. I'd been tuning
out most of this talk all my life, but I understood enough to
know that anybody claiming to be from a different dimension was either deeply disturbed or trying to punk me.

Once I got to school, I darted through the hallways like
some kind of nervous woodland creature. I half expected
the origami stalker to jump out at any moment, but nobody
gave any sign they'd pranked me. Most kids were busy put-
ting up posters and other decorations for the Student Showcase, an event I'd been dreading because it promised to
showcase all my failures. First a basketball game (where I'd
be benched), then a halftime routine with some songs from

the drama class musical (where I'd be stuck backstage), followed by the science fair (where I had no project).

As if the showcase and the stalker weren't enough stress, *voilà,* I found yet another note. It fell from the top shelf of my locker, poking me in the neck on its way down. A yellow-headed caracara, another fold I'd invented. All these notes were starting to remind me of the never-ending Hogwarts admission letters in the first Harry Potter book. Except they weren't funny.

With hands shaking once again, I unfolded the caracara and read the message inside:

Hi, Me,

At this point you're thinking, "This is just like all those Hogwarts admission letters at the beginning of Harry Potter." Why do I know you're thinking this? Because I would be too, and I'm you. Come to Me Con at the Janus Hotel South and find out how else we think alike.

Ours sincerely,
Me

Me Con? What sort of name was that? It sounded like a convention. A convention of . . . Mes?

"Hey," somebody said behind me.

I wasn't exactly relaxed to begin with, and being snuck up on didn't help. So I did what came naturally: I jumped in complete terror and bonked my head on the locker frame. "Ow!"

Twig laughed as I rubbed the sore spot, but I didn't mind. I liked her laugh and everything else about her. She had a round face that hid nothing and brown eyes that missed nothing. Her mountain of curly hair defied description because it took on a cool new shape every day. This particular morning she'd given herself a ponytail on top of her head and let the rest of her hair do what it pleased. It looked great, but I was too rattled to tell her that.

"Nice one!" she said. "What's that in your hand?"

I shoved the note into my pocket. I'd been friends with Twig since second grade and could tell her nearly anything, but this Me Con business was just too weird to talk about. Besides, if she was the one behind the prank, I wouldn't give her the satisfaction of knowing how much it had messed me up.

"Nothing!" I said.

Twig arched an eyebrow. Only three-quarters of an arch, not the hundred-percent arch she gave me when I really screwed up. "Whatever. So, did you watch what I posted last night?"

I'd been hoping she wouldn't bring that up.

Twig was big into her video channel and made a new post almost every day. Yeah, everybody has a channel on some app or another, but Twig's was different. Unlike other kids, who blathered on with their boring thoughts on video games or beauty tips, Twig did actual news stories. Sometimes even investigative journalism. Her post on corruption at the county fair got national coverage, mostly from the novelty of a thirteen-year-old girl exposing a bribery scheme at a farm-animal beauty pageant. She also attracted statewide attention for her report on school funding, though I personally didn't understand a word of it—maybe because I was the product of underfunded schools.

Other times Twig did commentary, giving her opinion on issues like climate change and voting rights. Her most recent post explored the pressure that gets dumped on middle schoolers, and I was pretty sure she was using me as an example: "I have this friend who's overwhelmed by the expectation to 'succeed' and 'achieve' something, and it's driving him up a wall. He thinks he has to have a 'thing,' something he's good at, to compete with other people. But in the end, all he's doing is competing with some impossible idea of himself. It's only making him miserable."

When I'd opened up to Twig about feeling like a failure, I didn't think she'd blab to the internet about it. Okay, technically she didn't blab, since she didn't use my name. Still, anybody who knew we were friends might have suspected she was talking about me.

I'd spent last night thinking up all kinds of nasty things

to tell her, but with this Me Con situation, her video was the farthest thing from my mind.

"It was okay, I guess," I said.

She was about to press me for more details, when an enormous kid appeared at my side, his huge frame blotting out the fluorescent light.

Nash, the seventh grade's most popular monster, had arrived to make my life even worse.

★ 3 ★

Nashed

"Hey, bro, how are ya?" Nash wrapped a thick arm around me, squeezing my shoulder blades against my spine.

Twig whipped out her phone and aimed its camera at Nash and me. What a couple we made: me with the bad hair and general scrawniness, him with the wavy black locks and action-figure physique. He looked like a statue of a magnificent soldier mounted on a horse. I looked like a goofy little pigeon taking a dump on the statue's head.

"Perfect!" said Twig. "Just act natural, you two. Do your thing. Don't mind me."

Nash smiled with the patience of a parent playing some stupid game with a kid. "What're you doing?"

"I'm working on an episode about the different faces we

wear. You know, how someone can have a lot of different sides to them. You're a perfect example, Nash. Can I interview you?"

"Uh, sure." Nash squeezed another year of life from my body.

"Great. Now, would you say that along with being an athlete, a top student, and a promising young actor, you also wear the hat of . . . a bully?"

Nash let go of me. I had to hunch over a little to catch my breath. "A bully?!" he said.

Twig kept the camera on him. "Isn't it true that you pretend you're being nice to Meade but you're actually messing with him? All the roughhousing, all the embarrassing extra attention. Isn't that more or less as bad as if you were to beat him up?"

Nash grabbed my arm in a vise grip and pulled me in for a bro-on-bro head rub. "I'm just horsing around with my good buddy!"

A pack of nearby kids snickered at this.

"Exactly," said Twig. "On the surface it sounds good, but aren't you really trying to be mean? What are your feelings on that?"

Nash forced a smile as he tightened his hold on my arm. "What do you think, Meade? Am I some kind of big bad meanie?"

What was I supposed to say? Twig was right. Nash was a stealth bully who worked his evil behind the scenes. But if I called him out on it, everybody would think I was a whiner.

I just couldn't win. And Twig had made it worse by bringing it up in the first place.

"Um, it's cool," I said.

"See?" said Nash. "We're just havin' fun! Thanks for including me in your show, Twig. Let me know when you post it."

Annoyed he hadn't taken the bait, Twig shoved the phone into her pocket and headed toward science. "Come on, Meade, let's get to class."

Nash wrapped his arm around me again, nearly fusing the bones and muscles in my back. That's when a strange fizzing spread through my body. At first I thought my limbs were falling asleep, but it was just the opposite. I felt stronger and tougher, not weaker. For a second there, I even thought I could break free of Nash if I tried. But I didn't. Whatever this was—adrenaline, stress reaction, nerve damage—it wouldn't help me. So I ignored the feeling until it went away.

"Actually we have some basketball team stuff to discuss," said Nash. "He'll be there in a sec."

Nash and I were teammates in name only. He was the captain; I barely got to play. Not that I cared: basketball was just another fake goal for the MeMinder, to keep Mom and Dad happy. They were thrilled to see me try a sport, even a sport I stank at.

"Meade?" said Twig, waiting for me to join her.

Our audience laughed again. Nash tried to shush them, but it didn't work. "What's so funny?" Nobody could miss the wink-wink in his voice, and they laughed harder.

I'd be facing even more embarrassment if I let Twig bail me out of this, so I played along with Nash. "Yeah, we'll be right there."

Sucking her teeth in frustration, Twig headed to science as Nash pulled me in the other direction. "Make way for my best bud, the coolest guy in school!" he shouted. The way he always bellowed to the world about how cool I was made me less cool every time.

I had no clue where Nash was taking me, but I knew it couldn't be anywhere good. The halls had mostly cleared by the time he dragged me to a door I'd always figured for a janitor's closet. He whipped out a key, made sure the coast was clear, then opened the door and pulled me inside.

I came face to face with shelves full of scientific grossness: bug displays, tubs of algae, and jars stuffed with dead snakes, frogs, and much worse floating in formaldehyde. Mr. Lunt sometimes trotted out these oddities for his lectures. They were disgusting enough in class, but flat-out horrific in this dark and tight space.

"This is Mr. Lunt's supply closet," Nash said, shutting the door. "I run errands for him, so I've got the key. Figure this is the perfect place to teach you a lesson about pranking your team captain."

I didn't want to face Nash just then, but it was either him or a jar of dead baby pigs soaking in alcohol. "What are you talking about?"

"You don't remember what you did to my homework? Every page of it folded up into those dumb little creatures you make all the time? You turned my research paper for Mr. Lunt into an entire zoo's worth of animals!"

"I didn't . . . I wouldn't!"

"Cut the bull! It was fancy origami. Who else but you folds paper like that?!"

I had a very strong suspicion about exactly who had done this. "Uh, these origami in your locker: did they have any, um, notes on the back?"

"No! But you knew that already, didn't you, Meade?! Because you're the one who made them!"

There could be only one reason somebody would turn Nash's homework into origami: sabotage. My stalker had folded Nash's research paper just to sic him on me.

Nash picked up a jar stuffed with four dead baby armadillos, each of them chalk white. "Did you know the armadillo is one of the few animals that have identical kids? Almost always four babies, quadruplets just about every time."

I hated how, on top of everything, Nash knew more than I did. It would be one thing if the kid who'd ruined my reputation and routinely threatened my very existence was just a dumb jock. But like Twig said, Nash had many sides. When he wasn't scoring the most points at every game, he was earning straight As, making music with his band, and generally "achieving" all over the place. He was the most well-rounded bully I could ever have hoped would pick on me. If I accomplished in a year just a tenth of what Nash accomplished all the time, Mom and Dad wouldn't bother me about the Achieve-O-Meter ever again.

"But I didn't bring you here to talk about armadillos," Nash continued. "Or even that stupid prank with my homework. We need to have a chat about Twig."

"Twig? What's she got to do with this?"

"I've seen the way you look at her. You want to be more than just her friend, don't you?"

He had me there. I used to just like Twig, but lately I'd started to *really* like her, as in like-like. The problem was I didn't know what to do about it. I hadn't realized until now that Nash liked her too.

Nash smirked. "Thought so. Remember, she and I are starring in the play together, so *I'm* her friend now. And that means you can't be."

So that was it. Nash saw me as a rival. No wonder he'd started picking on me more than usual lately. I knew for a fact that Twig didn't go for jocks like Nash, but this wasn't the best time to bring that up.

Nash stormed out of the closet. "Keep talking to her, and next time I'll find a place worse than Lunt's closet for you!"

He slammed the door, locked it with a loud click, and stomped away, leaving me alone in the dark with nothing for company but four identical dead armadillos and their chemically preserved friends.

18

★ 4 ★

Yeast Bomb

If there's one thing I'm good at, it's avoiding eye contact. But that wasn't a possibility in Mr. Lunt's science-specimen closet of horror. Tiny dead eyes, milky and unblinking, stared at me from the shelves. The armadillos especially skeeved me out. Four carbon-copy bodies stuck together forever in a lab jar. That's probably what Me Con would feel like—if it were real and not just some stupid prank.

I did my best to ignore all those dead animal eyes and focused on the door. It had an old lock, the kind a thief on some TV show might pick open with the right tools and know-how. If only I had tools and any kind of know-how. My only ticket out of here was to scream like a baby until someone came to my rescue.

I opened my mouth to get it all over with when the fizzing returned. It was the same sensation I'd felt at the lockers, but this time it buzzed in my hands, not my arms or legs. I twirled my fingers in the air, amazed at how light and nimble they'd become. They practically danced around with a mind of their own, so maybe it was their idea to pick the lock. All I knew for sure was that it suddenly seemed like the most natural thing in the world to shove a paper clip from my backpack into the lock and twist it around a few times until the door popped open.

I had no idea how I'd just pulled this off, and no time to think about it either. I jumped out of my prison and ran to class, nearly knocking over Mr. Clark, the janitor, on the way.

The MeMinder showed that I'd missed only five minutes of science. That was still long enough to get a nasty look from Mr. Lunt when I slunk into his room. I scurried to the lab counter I shared with Twig.

"Nash told me you had bathroom stuff to take care of after you two talked," Twig whispered as I took a seat. "Feeling sick or something?"

Nash, at the next counter, gave me the world's most menacing wink. I took the hint: any mention of what really had gone down and I was toast. So

I just shrugged and let Twig think I had diarrhea or whatever.

Twig plopped a small bowl of bubbling sludge in front of me. Yeast. We'd spent a very boring week in this room watching yeast bubbles clone themselves under a microscope. Copy after copy of the same yeast, over and over, nothing ever changing. If it weren't for the excitement of leaning in close to Twig as we shared the microscope, I'd have fallen asleep in here ages ago. Maybe that's what Me Con would be like, if it were real—everybody as boring as matching yeast bubbles, and without Twig around to break up the monotony.

"I went ahead and made today's specimens," she said. "Care to do the slides?"

"Yeast?! My favorite! You shouldn't have!"

Twig laughed, so of course Nash shot me a vicious look that no one but me noticed.

"We never talked about my latest episode," said Twig. "What did you think?"

My answer to this dreaded question would have to wait. On the lab counter, just beyond the bowl of yeast, I saw an origami white-mouthed mamba, yet another of my supposedly original creations. In a panic, I lunged for it, elbowing the bowl of yeast in the process. It sailed straight off the lab counter and splattered on Nash, coating him in a thick wad of goo.

The class went silent as Nash took in the mess all over himself.

"Sorry!" I said, knowing I was dead whether I apologized or not.

Nash laughed like this was all a big joke and paper-toweled himself dry. But the moment everybody got back to their lab work, he flashed me his most sinister *I'll kill you later* look.

I shoved the mamba in my pocket as Mr. Lunt made an announcement. "Let's spend the rest of class on final prep for your science fair projects. I'm sure you're all done. This is simply a chance for me to get a peek at your presentation and offer some feedback before tonight."

I hadn't expected to be put on the spot like this. Suddenly, yeast didn't sound so bad.

Nash shot up his hand and called Mr. Lunt over, showing him a poster crammed with all kinds of information about "The Impossible Pipe Dream of Cold Fusion." It only took a few seconds for Mr. Lunt to proclaim, "Nash! This is brilliant! It perfectly captures how cold fusion simply isn't possible."

"And Golden Boy does it again," said Twig.

"Well, he hasn't won yet."

She smirked. "So you've actually started on your project already?"

"It just so happens I have!"

"Geez, lighten up. I'm only joking."

I might have apologized, but Mr. Lunt appeared at my side. "And how's your project coming along, Meade?"

"Oh, it's great."

Mr. Lunt stared at me over the rims of his droopy glasses. The guy had it in for me. "Then, where are your notes?"

"Uh, I left them at home. Didn't think we'd need them today."

Naturally, the MeMinder chose this moment to butt in. "Begin science fair project immediately!" Its robot voice filled the room. "Project due this evening! Only one percent complete. Begin work immediately!"

Everybody laughed, even Mr. Lunt. "You should listen to that doohickey on your wrist," he said. "I guess we'll see what you cobble together by tonight."

Once Mr. Lunt had moved along to the next counter, Twig punched my sore shoulder hard enough to make me wince. This was her way of bucking up my spirits. "Don't worry, you'll think up something," she said. "You always do."

★ 5 ★

Benedict!

Out in the hall after class, I unfolded the mamba to read more unfamiliar words from a very familiar hand:

Hi, Me,

Nash giving you a hard time? I may have had something to do with that. Sorry, we Mes can't resist getting the better of that kid when we have the chance. You'll learn how to get the better of him too—at Me Con. You'll pick up tips from other Mes who've put their versions of that jerk in his place. You may even learn a thing or two about getting Mr. Lunt off your back, or getting

Twig interested in being more than your friend.
I'm telling you, it's the real deal. The Janus
South. After school. Be there.

Ours sincerely,
Me

Any kid at school could have written this note. Even people I'd never talked to knew me as the kid who got more attention than he wanted from Nash. And anybody who cared probably figured I had a thing for Twig. It was the most obvious letter so far, but also the one that really got me thinking. If there actually were different versions of me out there dealing with Nash and Twig—not to mention Mom and Dad—some of them were bound to have advice. It was a nice little fantasy to daydream about, at least.

The rest of the morning didn't go much better than the way it had started. The origami notes kept coming, all of them in shapes I'd thought were solely mine: a bat-eared fox under my desk in algebra, a Norwegian forest cat by the cafeteria's Build-a-Spud station, a stickleback gar shooting out of my saxophone in band, an Asian house shrew in my PE uniform. Whoever had left these creations knew my schedule right down to the bathroom breaks, if the alligator snapping turtle on the flusher of my go-to urinal was any indication.

Having a stalker was bad enough, but a stalker who stole my best origami ideas was even worse. And then

they'd rubbed it in my face by not even trying hard enough. Though these creations technically weren't bad, there was something a little too by-the-book about them, like whoever had made them wasn't having any fun.

The notes themselves got more and more wacky, but that also made them harder to resist. They tried to sell me on the same pitch about how Me Con was the solution to all my problems, the place for tips on improving my grades, doing better at band and basketball, becoming more popular, etc. A lot of them ended with the line "What kind of Me do you want to be?" The only Me I wanted to be was the kind who didn't get any more of those letters. But I still read and reread each one, searching for clues about who'd written them.

I got so absorbed in the mystery of it all that I was late for Ms. Assan's drama class. No big loss. There was nothing for me to do there anyway. I was Nash's understudy in *Benedict!,* a middle school version of the hit Broadway rap musical about Benedict Arnold, the notorious traitor of the Revolutionary War. Nash played the lead role, and I was supposed to memorize his lines in case he missed a show. The thing was, Nash, the perfect physical specimen, never got sick. That left me with nothing to do but sit through the rehearsal like always, watching Nash ham it up with Twig, who played Mrs. Arnold. As the two of them performed a flawless duet of "Call Us Mr. and Mrs. Traitor," I cursed myself for choosing "acting in a play" from the list of preprogrammed Achieve-O-Meter goals.

At least Nash was so busy with the play that I didn't have to worry about him getting revenge on me just yet. Instead, Twig cornered me backstage during her first break. "Seriously, why are you acting so cagey about last night's episode? What did you think of it?"

Any other day I might have lied, if only for the sake of our friendship, not to mention a lifelong fear of confrontation. But today wasn't any other day.

"You really want to know?"

"I've been waiting all this time."

The notes, the stalking, Me Con—it all swirled around in my head until the words spilled out: "It just would've been nice if you hadn't used me as an example of a loser to the entire internet."

Twig looked crushed. "I didn't call you a loser! I didn't call you anything! I didn't even use your name!"

"You might as well have!"

The backup dancers, dressed like minutemen and redcoats, started to stare. There's nothing drama kids like better than, well, drama.

Twig lowered her voice. "I've tried to talk to you for weeks about this stuff. This achievement nonsense, this need to have a 'thing.' It's just stressing you out."

"Easy for you to say! You've got your show and your acting. And now you've got Nash."

"What?! That's gross! Give me a break! You're just mad because you know I'm right."

Before she could say more, the MeMinder burst in on the conversation. "You must begin work on your science fair project now to achieve your goal! Student Showcase tonight!"

For once I appreciated the intrusion. "Sorry to cut this short, but the Achieve-O-Meter has spoken."

I headed for the school exit, leaving my former best friend behind. This was the final straw in a final-straw kind of day. I had a few classes left, but I needed to go out and do something stupid.

Breaking into an old abandoned hotel sounded like just the right kind of stupid.

★ 6 ★

The Hotel with Two Faces

It was kind of a letdown to break into a shuttered hotel and not even see a rat. Or ripped-up walls. Or boarded windows. Would a dark, shadowy corner have been too much to ask for? In the empty lobby of the Janus Hotel, the lights worked, the rugs were clean, and the walls barely had a ding. There wasn't even so much as a scratch on the wood paneling of the massive check-in desk.

That's not to say it wasn't scary. At the end of the day, even a well-kept abandoned hotel is still an abandoned hotel.

The lobby was a big cavern that hadn't been updated since the early nineties, when Mom and Dad met there. It looked silly with its fake-marble columns, cheesy red and blue neon lights, and black-and-white checkerboard floor. Above the doorway to the elevator bank hung the Janus logo, featuring a bearded guy with two faces staring in opposite directions. I sort of remembered Janus from a Percy Jackson book, a god of doorways or something. Did the Greeks have any idea how terrifying a guy with two faces would look in a big, empty place like this?

At least it hadn't been hard to break in. I couldn't get through the locked front doors with the FOR SALE sign on them, but one of the notes listed a passcode for the employee entrance off to the side. It had totally worked. If the origami stalker was right about the code, what else about their prank might turn out to be true? I still didn't believe in Me Con for a second, but the notes seemed a lot more legit now that they'd gotten me this far. If somebody had gone to this much trouble to bring me out here, there had to be something to see. Surely not a convention of my duplicates from parallel Earths, but something.

I stepped into the elevator bank and peeked down the long hallway. There wasn't any Me Con in that direction, just a big, empty ballroom. I noticed the green call button light on the elevator flickering on and off, like it didn't work right anymore. I edged closer, drawn to that light, almost hypnotized by it. Somewhere along the way, the fizz started up again, not in my arms or hands this time, but in my head. It gave me the sense that something bigger than an elevator car lay beyond those doors. Something much bigger, like when the lights go out at a planetarium and the ceiling fills up with stars. My brain knew the elevator probably didn't work anymore, but the rest of me wanted to see what would happen if I pressed the button. So I did.

The door rumbled open on a perfectly normal elevator car, just waiting for me to step in. Its speakers played some pop song from the 1980s that always made Mom and Dad groan when it came on the radio. The fizzing stopped and my head went back to normal. I figured it might just be a headache coming on. Then I saw the thing lying on the elevator floor.

An origami note.

This one was folded into a Eurasian three-toed woodpecker. I wanted so badly to know what the note inside said, but no way was I stepping into that contraption. Are the elevators even maintained when a building closes? What if the doors, once shut, wouldn't open again? What if the lifting cable snapped? What if this was all a trap laid by a psycho killer? It was time to turn back. This little adventure had already been exciting enough.

The rattle of keys nearby pulled me back to reality. Two janitors stood outside the hotel entrance, one of them unlocking the door. They hadn't seen me yet, but it was only a matter of time before they did—there wasn't so much as a garbage can to hide behind in the entire hotel.

That left only one way to go. I stepped into the elevator and looked for the Close button. That was no easy feat, since the control panel went all the way up to ninety-nine. Why would a hotel with only a few floors need an elevator with so many numbers? Maybe the origami stalker would tell me what to do. I snatched up the paper woodpecker on the floor and read the note inside:

Hey, Me,

Sorry to send you here during the monthly cleaning for prospective buyers, but you needed the motivation. I know the elevator looks scary, but seriously, I've done all the convincing I can about Me Con. Now it's up to you. I promise you won't regret it. Or you might, but at least it'll be interesting. Just press the button for zero. Trust me.

Ours sincerely,
Me

So that was it—this was all a setup. How could I have been so stupid?

A floor polisher whirred in the lobby. The cleaners had gotten right to work, and any second now they'd reach the elevator bank. I chose danger over getting busted: I found the Close button and pressed it.

Nothing happened. Stupid broken elevator.

I jabbed at the next button over, the one for the first floor. This time, it worked. The ring around the button lit up with a green glow, and the door rumbled shut. Only then did I remember that the note had said to press the button for zero.

Oh well, it wasn't like this old crate could move anyway. I was lucky the door had even closed.

All I had to do now was wait inside a few minutes until the janitors made their way past the elevator bank. Once they reached the ballroom, I'd sneak back out, sprint to my bike, and hightail it home.

The last thing I expected was for the elevator to shudder to life. Even worse, it started moving. I looked around for a kill switch, a reverse setting, a reset key, anything.

Nothing.

All I could do was stand there and wait to see where this ride wound up.

★ 7 ★

Now You See Me

You'd think an elevator with a hundred glowing green buttons would shoot into the air like the glass elevator at the end of *Charlie and the Chocolate Factory*. But the Janus elevator rode like any other—smooth and slow, with just a few bumps here and there. That didn't stop my insides from puddling at the thought of where I'd end up when it stopped.

If it stopped.

I had the distinct feeling of dropping, but the place didn't have a basement that I knew of, so that couldn't have been right. After what felt like forever, the car slowed to a halt and the door slid open. I took a deep breath and peered out to see . . . the very same elevator bank I'd left behind just a second before. I hadn't moved at all; it had just felt like I had.

Stupid busted elevator.

At least there was no sign of the cleaners now. They must have gone deeper into the hotel. This was my best chance to sneak away. I rushed to the lobby and made a beeline through the side exit. But my relief disappeared in a poof as soon as I saw the bike rack.

Empty.

My bike and its lock were gone. This wasn't the safest neighborhood in town, but come on, what kind of jerk steals a crappy old kid's bike in broad daylight? Now I had to walk home.

I was so caught up in worrying about what Mom and Dad would say that I didn't pay much attention to the world around me. Then I noticed the Kentucky Fried Chicken on the corner. It looked just like the regular old KFC that had been there forever, but the sign now read KENTUCKY FRIED FISH AND CHIPS, and posters in the window hawked haggis, black pudding, and bangers and mash.

I gazed at the sign for a long time to make sure my eyes weren't playing tricks on me. Other than the name, nothing else had changed—same parking lot, same drive-thru lane, same cloud of cooking grease hovering overhead. I figured it must have been some kind of joke, the work of street artists pulling a prank. But no one driving by gave the sign a second glance. Maybe I wouldn't have noticed either if I hadn't been on foot. Or maybe I was extra sensitive to practical jokes now that I was on the butt end of one. Thing is, KFC wasn't the only business that had changed on this street. The Dick's Sporting Goods had become Spotted Dick's Sporting Goods, with the soccer gear in its window display advertised as FOOTBALL SUPPLIES. A few doors down, the 7-Eleven sold "crisps" instead of potato chips, and "petrol" instead of gas. And the old patriotic army surplus store flew a UK flag instead of its usual American one.

Since when had British stuff gotten so big?

Two men stepped out of a Royal Navy where an Old Navy used to be. They were dressed up like well-to-do gentlemen from American Revolution times: ruffled silk shirts, lacy frills, long-tailed coats, and knickers. Even powdered wigs. I figured they might have been headed to a costume party, until I saw other men and women wearing clothes from the same period. They spoke with British accents to boot. It was like a bunch of extras from some low-budget History Channel documentary had stepped off the screen and taken over the neighborhood.

As I tried to make sense of all this, a bus pulled up to the curb—a red double-decker bus like the ones people ride in London. It carried an ad banner featuring the Statue of Liberty, but she wore a fur-trimmed cape instead of robes and held a scepter instead of a torch. Her pointy crown had turned puffy and round, with diamonds stuck all over. VISIT NEW YORK, it read, and GOD SAVE THE QUEEN!

When the bus pulled away, the store it had blocked came into view. It was a sleek space with big windows show-

casing state-of-the-art phones, computers, and other gadgets. Nothing sur-
prising there, but the big, stylized ME
above the door looked just like the
logo Dad used for Me Co. I sprinted
across the street for a closer look.
Inside were MeMinders in totally
new shapes, sizes, and colors, plus a
whole line of MePhones, MePads, and
MeLaptops I'd never seen before.

This could mean only one thing: someone had stolen
Dad's company and made it a whole lot bigger.

I was reaching for my phone to call him when a little
white pyramid in the window whirred to life. A label underneath it read SECUREME: IT'S A CAMERA. IT'S A PROJECTOR. IT'S
SECURE. The lens in the middle of the pyramid shot out a
hologram of Dad right beside me on the sidewalk. He wore a
stylish black colonial outfit and white powdered wig. I could
only watch in petrified silence as a sleek holo-car pulled up
beside Holo-Dad, its door sliding open to reveal no one in
the driver's seat. "The Self-Driving MeCar from Me Corp.,"
Holo-Dad said with a British accent. "Let life drive you."

Why had I never heard of holographic commercials?
Why would anybody put Dad in one? And when had he
picked up that accent and those clothes? When I left the
house that morning, Dad had been wearing jeans and a
Dungeons & Dragons T-shirt. He was an adult nerd, not
some kind of actor.

I turned to the street and saw a MeCar like the one in the ad waiting at the stoplight. It had no driver, just a family relaxing in the seats. A living room on wheels. The kids stared at MePads, the mom talked on a MePhone, and the dad made notes on holographic paper projecting from a Me-Minder on his wrist. When the light changed, they didn't even look up as the robot car whisked them away.

And just like that, it all came together in my head. Self-driving MeCars. Colonial fashion. British accents. Kentucky Fried Fish and Chips. The Statue of Royalty in New York. Me Corp. instead of Me Co.

This wasn't my home.

The origami stalker hadn't lied. There really was a multiverse. And I'd traveled through it to another Earth.

★ 8 ★

Walk a Mile in My Shoes

I've never been able to fantasize about adventures on other worlds without worrying over all the little things that could go wrong. I can handle the idea of rampaging dragons or evil sorcerers in a magical fantasyland, but not the disgusting medieval diseases floating around, like trench mouth. Killer robots and deadly aliens in some futuristic setting? No problem. But with my luck, space travel would make me barfy. And if those things didn't do me in, I figure my general incompetence surely would. I'd probably just become a sitting duck for whatever wanted to eat, enslave, or dissect me.

That's why this parallel reality was so great: beyond the accents, the clothes, and the fact that Dad ran a megacorporation, it felt familiar, like going to another country that spoke English.

I was looking around to see where to start exploring, when one of the robot cars broke away from the robot traffic and stopped in front of me. The rear door slid open, and Nash, of all people, leaned out. He wore stupid colonial clothes like everybody else, but the sight of him still gave me chills.

"Hullo, mate!" he said, so friendly it almost sounded genuine. This Nash must have been a better actor than my Nash.

"Uh, hey."

"I was just headed back to school for the showcase. You too?" The showcase on my Earth wasn't scheduled to start for another few hours. I guessed they did things early here. "Where's your ride?"

He must have thought I was the Me who lived on this Earth. Up until then, I hadn't even considered that another edition of me would be out there. Maybe this world wasn't so safe after all. Plus, it was freaky hearing Nash with a British accent.

"Just thought I'd walk." I tried to sound casual.

Nash slapped his palms together. "Need a lift, then, mate? It'd be right proper to take you! Unless you want to keep walking, which I would totally understand. But time's ticking!"

The idea of running into the legit Me of this reality must have really done a number on me, because I didn't think twice about getting into a robot car with British Nash. Only when I sat beside him and the door slid shut did I realize I was trapped. By then it was too late.

"Car, continue trip." As the car zipped back into the street, Nash gave my clothes the once-over. "That's really authentic!" He didn't sound sarcastic, but excited for real. "Are we all supposed to wear costumes for the showcase?"

Oh, right, my T-shirt and jeans. On this Earth, *I* was the one in the costume, not vice versa. Fashion must have taken a different path here, along with US history and fast food.

"Uh, my suit got dirty on the way here, so I had to change into the only thing I could find. Got it at a costume store."

Nash sighed with relief. "Let me order you a new suit, then. I'd be honored. What size are you? Pisces?"

"Pisces?"

"Hullo? The zodiac size chart?" He chuckled, but in a nice way. "I figure you're somewhere between Pisces and Aries. Maybe you're a cusp?"

I didn't know what else to do but nod. A size chart based on the zodiac? This Earth got weirder by the second.

Nash spoke into a MeMinder on his wrist. "I need a Chip Chip Cheerio in size Pisces. Make that a Pisces-Cusp. And with extra ruffles." He beamed at me. "There you go, mate, all set to deliver."

"Right. Thanks. Uh, I'll pay you back."

Nash laughed like I'd made a joke. "Somehow I bloody well think the richest bloke in the United States of the British Empire is good for it."

"You mean the United States of America?"

He snorted. "Good one! I almost missed that question on our history test last week."

"Come again?"

"You know, the way they called the colonies America until the Colonial Uprising went all to pot and they changed the name."

The American Revolution had failed here? It was a fascinating idea, but not as fascinating as the other thing he'd said.

"I'm, uh, rich?"

Nash doubled over with laughter. "Stop, mate! You're killing me!"

Now that he'd mentioned it, of course the Me of this world would have a lot of money. Any kid whose dad owned Me Corp. would be loaded. From the car window, I saw the company logo all over the place. On billboards hawking MeMail, MeDocs, MeMaps, and "the whole family of Me-Apps." On shopfront signs that read Follow Us on MeBook and TwitMe. At an even bigger MeStore, which sold the full range of Me Corp. products, including a lot full of MeCars.

"Something on your mind?" said Nash, snapping me back to the conversation. "I can only imagine what must be on your plate right now. But at least you don't have to worry about the science fair, eh? Got that in the bag, I expect."

"Do I?"

He wagged a finger at me. "Cheeky monkey! Don't make me crease up again!"

"Am I missing something?" I asked.

"Oh, stop already! By the way, you got a cold? You sound a bit off."

Oops, the accent. I put on my standard British voice, the one I used when reciting *Horrible Histories* skits with Twig. "Yes, my nose is a mite stuffy, ol' chap."

Nash squinted at me, then chuckled. This bad imitation of my archnemesis sure was jolly, I had to give him that. The car pulled into the school parking lot and dropped us off near the front entrance. "Here we are," he said, still chuckling. "Imagine, me giving you a ride. I'm chuffed! Oh, speaking of that."

He twiddled with his phone until it projected a hologram of the school basketball team in the air. It looked just like the team photo we'd taken back on my Earth, except for the lace frills on the uniforms. And instead of standing nearly out of the frame like I had in the original picture, I was front and center, holding up an obscenely large COLONIAL CRICKET CHAMPIONS trophy, as if I'd had something to do with winning it.

"What a day that was, mate." Nash beamed. "Been a week and I'm still wrapping my head around it. Colonial champions, and all thanks to you! You were cracking! And to think you took up cricket only six months ago! I've been training my whole life and can't hold a candle to you!" Nash's smile tightened for just a second. This Nash was better than mine at playing nice, but years of experience had taught me to watch out for cracks in the disguise. A tight smile was definitely a warning sign.

I scooted as far from him as possible. With no witnesses

43

around, he could get away with murder. Nash reached into his pocket, and I tensed up, but he just pulled out a stylus. "I know this is daft of me, but can you sign the team holo? I want to remember this forever."

In a daze, I took the stylus but didn't know what to do next. Nash tittered. "Feeling a little over-egged? I get it. That was one emotional day. Maybe you could just sign the spot near your head."

I reached out and wiggled the stylus in the air until it made something like my signature. "Cool!" I said.

"Yeah, I really like your latest update to the stylus editing software. Writes a lot smoother now. Oh, and while I've got you here." Nash fiddled with the phone again, and a new hologram appeared: a program for a historical rap musical called *Washington!* As in, George. Nash flipped the pages, stopping at the cast list. My picture was at the top, next to the words *George Washington, leader of a failed rebellion and traitor to mother England. Played by Meade Macon.*

"What a hit!" said Nash. "You really brought the house down! Mind signing this too?"

I air-wrote my signature again, more confused than ever. This upgraded model of me was captain of the best middle school cricket team and star of the school play on top of everything else? At this point I was starting to hate him.

As soon as we stepped out of the car, something swooped down from above and hovered in my face. I flinched before realizing it was a drone. A MeDrone, naturally. It plopped a box straight into my hands. "Delivery complete," the drone said in a British robot voice. I stared openmouthed as it hovered there like it was waiting for me to do something.

"Confirm purchase, please," it finally said.

"Oh, right." I opened the box to find a colonial-style suit like everyone else wore.

"Uh, looks good," I told the drone. "Purchase . . . confirmed?"

The drone's front section dipped as if bowing to me before it flew away.

"Brilliant!" Nash eyed my new duds as the car parked itself down the street. "Looks smashing!"

"Thanks. It was really thoughtful of you to get this."

Nash lowered his eyes, looking sheepish. "Least I could do for the hard time I used to give you when we were little tykes. I truly am sorry about that, mate. I was a right git back in my bullying days. But you helped me see the error of my ways, and I'm grateful for that."

"No problem." So this Nash had been a bully too, once upon a time. That meant the Me of this world hadn't always led such a charmed life after all. Had he always been rich? When had little Me Co. grown into ginormous Me Corp.? So many questions.

Nash cleared his throat. "Yeah, color me grateful. Though I can't say I'm grateful for what you did to my research paper this morning. Ha ha! Right proper joke! But hey, that was some bloody fine origami you made out of it. I'll decorate my bedroom with your art, most like!"

"Uh, my pleasure?"

For just a moment, I saw a hint of anger flash across Nash's face, but it passed and he was all smiles again. He pointed to a souped-up porta-potty with MeLoo on the side. "You can change in there. One of your more useful inventions, am I right? I'll just wait out here."

"It's cool—you don't have to." I hoped to make a break for it as soon as he left. If I played my cards right, I could get back to the hotel and home to my Earth in under a half hour.

"Oh, I insist." Was that a hint of menace in his voice? Or did I just not trust any Nash, no matter how much he smiled?

As soon as I stepped inside the MeLoo, a robot voice asked if I wanted a loo, a shower, a massage, a tan, or any of the other services it offered. I told it no thanks and got to work squeezing into the suit. Without a bag to carry my T-shirt and jeans, I had to leave them on underneath, which made for a tight fit. Once I snapped my buckles and arranged my ruffles (a little know-how I picked up from helping with costumes backstage at *Benedict!*), I stepped out of the MeLoo dressed more or less like everyone else. That didn't stop people from staring as I followed Nash into the school gym.

After all the whacked-out things I'd seen on this Earth so far, walking past the usual cruddy science fair projects kids made year after year felt like a comforting taste of home. Potato clocks, baking soda volcanoes, and endless experiments with magnets, mold, soda, eggs, and yeast. The posters screamed out the kinds of pointless questions people only ever bother to ask at science fairs: "How does salt water affect gummy bears?" "Do plants like music?" "Is yawning contagious?"

As I made my way through the gym, dead ringers for kids from my Earth whispered about me in their British accents. I checked to see whether I'd made some kind of eighteenth-century fashion no-no, like tying my cravat the wrong way. But I hadn't left a single piece of lace out of place. It had to be something else. Panic flooded my veins—maybe my double, the real Me of this Earth, had shown up already, and people here were confused to see us in the same place twice. Even worse, the Mom and Dad of this Earth might show up at any minute. They'd recognize me as an impostor in no time.

"Why so shy today?" Nash asked. "It's just your adoring public."

So that was it: I was famous. British Me must have attracted stares all the time. I never realized how nerve-racking that kind of attention could be, especially when I hadn't earned it.

I was seconds from fleeing the room, when someone behind me yelled, "Hey! I got your invite!"

It was Twig, speaking in the same British voice she used for recaps of *Doctor Who* episodes. With her rainbow-colored colonial suit and gravity-defying hair, she stood out from the crowd here as much as she did in my universe. "I got your holo-message, and the dance sounds scrummy!" She gave me a fist bump. "We haven't chummed around in forever, which is barmy! I can't wait to go as friends!"

"Uh, great." My annoyance with the Me of this world ticked up several more notches. On top of everything else, he'd gotten Twig to go out with him too? Even if it sounded more like a friend-date than a date-date, taking Twig to a dance was way above and beyond anything I'd ever managed. Still, a little part of me was relieved Twig didn't seem to worship him the way everyone else did. No matter what Earth she came from, Twig could never be a suck-up.

Nash walked up behind us, his face a mask of jealous rage. That is, until he caught me looking. Then he switched back to chip-chip-cheerio Nash, my best British mate. But he didn't fool me. This Nash hated my doppelgänger even more than my Nash hated me. I might have felt the same if I'd been a golden boy forced to play second fiddle to the smartest, richest kid in the world.

"Sorry to interrupt," Nash said, "but Mr. Lunt's about to announce the winner!"

Lunt stepped up to the mic stand in the center of the room, holding the trophy I'd always wanted so badly. "There he is!" He beamed at me like I was his best student. "I must say, Meade Macon, you've really outdone yourself this year!

Not only have you proven that cold fusion is quite possible, but you've also made it cheap and portable! Your MeFusion device will revolutionize the world! That's why Meade takes the top prize as this year's science fair winner!"

Cheers filled the gym. I looked around to make sure Lunt wasn't talking about someone else. Everybody whooped it up like I'd just made the best joke ever. It felt weird to have people laughing *with* me instead of *at* me. It felt even weirder taking the trophy, considering how a much better Me than myself had done all the work. But I staggered up to Lunt anyway.

"Speech!" yelled Nash. "Speech!"

Lunt thrust the trophy and the mic into my hand. My mind went blank. I'd never had to give a victory speech, because I'd never been victorious. What could I possibly say? *Thanks, everybody. My alternate self couldn't make it tonight, but I've come from a parallel Earth to accept this award on his behalf.* Somehow I didn't think that would fly with this crowd.

Just then the emergency exit doors creaked open, and a kid in a glittery green colonial suit entered the gym. He wore a paste-on beard and a monocle squished into his eye, but the disguise didn't fool me. I'd know that face anywhere. I saw it in the mirror every day.

He was me—the Me of this world. The rightful owner of the life (and science fair trophy) I'd just stolen.

And he wanted it all back.

49

★ 9 ★

Me in the Mirror

My living, breathing clone jerked his head toward the exit, the universal sign for *Time to go*. I looked around for another way out, but too many people stood between me and the front entrance. No choice. I had to leave with him.

"Well, duty calls!" said Lunt, taking the mic from my hand. "Let's have another round of applause for Meade Macon, everybody!"

As Twig, Nash, and the rest of the crowd cheered, I followed my spitting image out the door, fully expecting him to beat me up the first chance he got. Instead, he led me to a robot limo. "Door!" he ordered. The passenger door obeyed, sliding open.

"After you, Meticulous," he said.

Figuring *Meticulous* for some sort of British nickname, like *mate* or *old chap,* I crouched inside and took one of the back seats, plopping the trophy next to me. It was a sleek ride, with a leather interior, a flat-screen, a mini soda fountain, and a snack tray stuffed with British crisps and candy bars.

"To the office," the other Me commanded. He sat across from me, and the car glided into the traffic ahead.

The Me popped the monocle out of his eye and pulled off his costume beard. Now he looked just like me, except with one of those fake-messy hairstyles that probably took him an hour to get right. "Fiddlesticks!" he shouted. "Sorry for swearing, it's just—that was so exciting! How was my disguise? Guess I picked up a few things having my makeup done every day for *Baker's Dozen.* Who would have thought you could learn anything useful on the set of a sitcom?"

"Uh, yeah, great." I barely registered what he'd just said. Turns out that talking to yourself is more than a little distracting. It's even worse than listening to your own voice mail greeting.

"And how's my accent? Getting better, right? ''Ello, mate! I'm just your average citizen of the United States of the British Empire, guv'na!' It's all in the acting, you know. They don't call me Hollywood Me for nothing. Jumpin' Jehoshaphat, what a rush! Oh, me and my dirty mouth again! Sorry!"

"That's okay." I hadn't expected the conversation to go anything like this. Hollywood Me didn't sound like the wealthy, brilliant, multitalented popular kid I'd built up in my mind. He sounded more like an idiot.

"Bet you're glad the science fair's over," Hollywood continued. "Nice job winning that prize, by the way."

"Oh, thanks." Why was he congratulating me for winning his prize? This whole situation made less and less sense by the second.

"Sorry I had to get you out of there. When you didn't reply to my texts, I saw the science fair on your calendar and figured you might have been at school. I don't get it. You're like a gosh-darned genius, if you'll pardon my French. Why not just take the test that graduates you out of school early? Heck, you probably don't even need to do that. You could just jump straight to a college degree!"

"Uh, it's complicated."

Hollywood gave me a sly grin. "Because of Twig, right? I get it. There's a Twig on my world too. Holy cow, is she worth sticking around for! Oops, sorry. There I go again with my potty mouth!"

His world? Of course! Hollywood was a Me from a different Earth, just like myself. He came from a place where they didn't dress or talk like British people from 250 years ago. Apparently, they had a different definition of swearing too.

"Man, you've really carved out a nice life for yourself here, Meticulous," said Hollywood. That name again. Meticulous. Meticulous Me? Was that what the Me of this reality called himself? "Thanks for inviting me to be your assistant."

"Hey, the pleasure's all mine."

Hollywood gushed as he opened up a calendar app on the flat-screen. "It's just a light schedule today, but the big meeting with those reps from the China–Russia–North Korea Democratic Union is in a few hours. And of course you've got the board of directors' get-together in thirty minutes. After that you have the fund-raiser for the Justin Bieber Senate reelection campaign, followed by the concert."

"Concert? Who's playing again? I forgot."

Hollywood looked confused. "You are. With your band? Origami Drive?"

Meticulous fronted a band on top of everything else? What couldn't this overachieving jerk do?

The limo stopped at a street dominated by a gleaming office tower of glass and metal. I could make out the Me Corp. logo way up at the tiptop, glinting in the sun. An entire skyscraper reserved just for a company that Dad had built. I stared at it in awe until Hollywood nudged my elbow. This must have been where we were supposed to get out.

Strapping on his stupid beard and squinting into his monocle again, Hollywood ordered the limo to the parking garage, picked up the trophy, and led me into the busy Me Corp. lobby. We breezed past security guards who tipped their tricornered hats at us, and a crowd of employees stepped out of our way. I followed Hollywood into an elevator with a sign that read RESERVED FOR CEO.

Hollywood pressed the button for the hundredth floor, and up we went, not making any stops until we reached the top. The doors opened on a fancy office suite made of metal, glass, and polished concrete. An assistant appeared on my left to give me a purplish-green smoothie while an assistant on my right handed me a stack of MePads. Before I could so much as say thanks, Hollywood dumped the trophy on them and dragged me to the corner office with CEO on the door.

Dad wasn't in the office, but I could imagine him telling me not to touch anything there. The place was crammed with paintings and sculptures good enough for a museum. Even the metallic desk seemed like a work of art. When I took a few steps for a closer look, a holographic projector switched on, shining a nameplate in the air: MEADE MACON.

Dad wasn't in charge of Me Corp. I was. That is, the Meticulous Me of this reality. My dad wouldn't even let me run the dishwasher without supervision. How did Meticulous get to run a whole corporation as CEO?

Hollywood lingered at the door but didn't come in. "You seem a little off, or 'knackered,' as they might say here on this Earth. Want me to help you prep for the meeting? The board of directors is all hot and bothered for a progress report on the MindMe app you promised last quarter. I wrote up some excuses for the delay, the usual spiel about the tricky science of artificial intelligence and stuff like that. And I forced the RocketMe team to dream up some preliminary design specs for the spacecraft, just to give the board something to look at. Oh, you should also know that the initial medical test results on MendMe totally bombed. Absolutely no improvement in the patients. So we've got to figure out something positive to report there too."

"Uh, thanks. I'll be fine. Just need a minute."

"Okay." Hollywood looked far from certain. "See you in a few."

As soon as Hollywood shut the door, I looked around for a way out. I tried a door on the other side of the room and found a bathroom bigger than my living room back home. It had a shower, a tub, and a separate Jacuzzi, but no exit.

I was trapped.

I walked back to the desk and plopped myself in the chair, which molded to my body like I'd sat in it a zillion times. In a way, I had. Meticulous didn't have much in the way of personal stuff on his desk, save for a tidy row of fancy pens lined up perfectly. The only thing close to resembling clutter was a small metal tray off to the side that held a pile of origami. Most were failed attempts at origami octopuses, each of them lopsided, flat, or just plain mangled. I could sympathize. I knew all too well how hard it was to fold an octopus. As I rummaged through the pile and detangled their arms, I found other origami creations: a cobra, a honey badger, a caracara, and all the shapes from the notes that had haunted me back home. Was Meticulous the origami stalker? It was hard to imagine a preteen CEO with his own rock band taking time out to deliver some notes in my rinky-dink universe.

My hand must have made a gesture or touched some hidden switch on the desk, because another hologram sprang to life: a life-size bust of Mom spinning in the air. A banner underneath read IN MEMORIAM.

The Mom of this Earth was dead?

I wasn't so jealous of Meticulous Me anymore. As the hologram winked out, I thought about how I'd trade all the trophies and money and dates with Twig in the world for Mom. Losing her was unthinkable.

Mostly just to take my mind off wondering how this world's Mom had died, I snooped around the drawers, which unlocked at my touch. There wasn't much in them beyond files, but I did find another origami octopus, the most decent attempt yet. When I picked it up for a closer look, I saw that it covered a small holo-projector with a flash drive stuck in the side. This had to be something important, but I didn't have time to find out what. Voices approached from outside.

"But I left you in the office just now!" Hollywood was whining to someone. "Are you telling me you don't remember? It was only a few doggone minutes ago! Oops, sorry for swearing."

"I've been at the lab this whole bloody time!" said a familiar voice.

It was my voice. Our voice. An authentic British replica of our voice. That could mean only one thing.

The real Meticulous Me had returned.

★ 10 ★

Corporate Raider

I yanked the flash drive from the projector, stuffed it into my pocket, and raced to the bathroom. It was a suicidal place to hide if Meticulous were to take a leak, but where else could I run?

Crouching, dead quiet, I peeked through the crack in the door as another walking ditto mark of me strutted into the room. Meticulous Me wore a charcoal-gray colonial outfit and a super-serious look on his face. He stood so ramrod straight I felt slouchy by comparison. Everything about this Me screamed "uptight." Hollywood scurried in behind him.

"Are you off your trolley, Hollywood?!" Meticulous walked over to his desk, and my nerves seized up. Was he looking for the flash drive I'd just swiped?

"Great Caesar's ghost!" said Hollywood. "Excuse the language, but this is very frustrating! I swear I picked you up from school! Remember the science fair? The trophy?"

Meticulous grabbed the stack of MePads I'd left behind. "Like I care about some daft science fair? Next time you make a right mess of things, don't bloody well hide it with some childish prank." He headed for the door. "Grow up or I'll find myself another assistant."

Hollywood stuck out his tongue at Meticulous's back as he followed behind him.

Once they'd left together, I crept across the office and opened the door enough to peek out. The coast was clear. At least, I thought it was. When I swung the door wider, I nearly bonked it into none other than Mr. Clark, the janitor from school. He'd ditched his denim work clothes for an expensive colonial business suit, like the other executives here wore. This version of Mr. Clark must have had some sort of important muckety-muck position with Me Corp.

"Sir!" he said. "So glad I caught you. I'm just back from the Socialist Republic of Atlantis and need to talk to you about a few issues that came up there before the board meeting."

I didn't stop walking. "Save it for later, okay?"

"But, sir!"

"Later!"

I power-walked toward the elevator, mopping up my forehead sweat with a floppy silk sleeve as everybody gave me double takes. They must have just seen the real Meticulous pass by a few minutes before. Nothing I could do about that now. Only a few steps away from the elevator, I passed a conference room with big plate-glass windows and a bunch of people stuffed inside. This had to be the board of directors' meeting, where the real Meticulous and Hollywood had gone.

I covered my face with my hand and tried not to look too obvious going past. It worked. Almost. I'd just cleared the last window when Meticulous shouted loud enough that his words carried through the glass: "Are you questioning my ability to run this company?!"

When you hear yourself telling off somebody, it's impossible not to stop and have a look.

In the room, Meticulous stood before a table of stern-looking adults. The sternest of them shouted right back at Meticulous. It was none other than Ms. Assan, the drama teacher. She'd ditched her usual aging-hipster outfit for a colonial power suit. "If you don't start producing results again, we may have to rethink your running this company. Where's the MindMe AI prototype you promised? Why isn't RocketMe ready? And how come there's been not a peep on this life-extension device you've been going on about from the MendMe team?"

"They're coming!" yelled Meticulous. "These things take time! Can't you see that?!"

I was so amazed to see myself shouting back to a

grown-up that I almost missed Hollywood. He sat up in his seat near the window, looking from me to Meticulous and back again, awareness sinking in.

Busted.

I sprinted the rest of the way to the elevator and pounded the call button as Hollywood rushed out of the conference room. "Hey, get the fudge over here!" He ran toward me just as the door slid open. I hopped inside and punched CLOSE over and over until the door finally started rolling shut. Hollywood reached me and tried to shove his hand through the narrowing gap, but he was too late. "Security!" he shouted, the elevator closing in his face.

I pressed the button for the parking garage and treated myself to a long, deep breath. Maybe I could find the limo that had brought me here, or sneak away on foot. Either way, I had to get off this Earth and never come back.

★ II ★

Reckless Driving

Trapped in a strange world. On the run from a dim-witted rendition of myself. Feeling itchy and sweaty in frilly clothing. Maybe I shouldn't have skipped school after all.

As soon as the doors opened on the parking garage, I spotted Meticulous's limo in the RESERVED FOR CEO space in front of me. Only when I grabbed for the handle did I remember I didn't have the keys. I yanked at it anyway. "Open up already!"

A red light under the handle pulsed along my palm, and the limo's robot voice piped up. "Acknowledged. Welcome back, sir." The locks clicked and the doors swung open.

Before I could hop in, a pair of arms wrapped around me from behind. Hollywood Me.

"No idea how you got to this gosh-darned world, but you messed with the wrong gosh-darned Me!" He tightened his grip, which didn't feel much stronger than mine. "I trained in all forms of martial arts for my role in *Pallin' with the Shaolin*! So don't even think about it!"

I didn't know the first thing about wrestling, and neither did Hollywood. It was easy to break free of his hold, but he didn't give up. He came at me again, and we went at it some more, sliding along the side of the limo. Our identical bodies got so tangled together we must have looked like conjoined twins.

Just before we reached the back bumper, I managed to twist Hollywood around so his head hovered over the trunk. "Trunk!" I yelled.

Nothing happened.

Hollywood smirked. "You're on British soil. They call trunks *boots*."

"Boot!" I screamed.

The lid swung up, barely missing the back of Hollywood's head. "Hey!" he cried, letting go. "That almost hit me!"

I'd been hoping the lid would knock him out, but I guess that sort of thing only happens in movies. Now I needed a new idea, because wrestling was getting us nowhere. As Hollywood came at me, I shot my hand at his neck . . . and tickled him. There was a particular patch of skin just under the left side of my jaw that never failed to seize up my entire body whenever Mom, Dad, or Twig got me there. Something told me Hollywood might have that weak spot too.

I guessed right. As soon as I touched him there, Hollywood squealed with laughter and curled up his body, shielding himself against more tickling. That left him unprepared for the shove that came next. I pushed his unbalanced body into the empty *boot,* just wide and deep enough to fit an obnoxious Me. I tucked in his feet with one hand and slammed the lid shut with the other.

I wasn't too keen on taking a limo with my look-alike screaming in the back, so I searched around for some other ride. In the next space sat a sleek red MeScooter sipping power from a charging box. It was so beautiful I couldn't resist reaching out and touching it. A red light inside the handlebar grip scanned my hand, and the bike hummed to life.

"Welcome, sir," said the scooter's robot voice. "Fancy a ride?"

The scooter moved like butter on wheels, racing me far from Me Corp. headquarters in a matter of minutes. It was so fun to ride, I almost forgot I was supposed to be making a getaway.

At a stoplight, I tried to figure out the fastest way to the Janus. A robot voice blared behind me: "Citizen, please move forward!" The words blasted from a MeCar convertible behind me. Rattled, I backed into the car's bumper, setting off its alarm. "Collision! Collision!" I turned all the way around for a better look. An old lady snoozed in the back seat, oblivious to the racket.

A British-style police siren split the air a block away. Great, cops were the last thing I needed. I cranked the throttle and zoomed off.

Turns out it's not so hard being chased in a world of self-driving cars. The robots were programmed to follow the rules of traffic, but Meticulous's scooter let me drive however I pleased. I buzzed past countless cars obeying the speed limit without fail, their robot voices nagging me:

"Citizen! No weaving between cars!"

"Citizen! No running a stop sign!"

"Citizen! No going the wrong way down a one-way street!"

Their warnings scared me at first, until I realized the cars and the people they carried couldn't do a thing about it.

But despite all my darting and dodging, the siren grew louder and louder. I looked back and saw the robot cars turn aside like a wave to make room for the police cruiser. The cop behind the wheel drove with no robotic aid. That meant she could bend the rules of traffic, just like me.

"Pull over!" her partner shouted through a speaker.

Even if I'd wanted to pull over, how could I ever explain myself? I kept going. Before too long I reached the sketchy warehouse district at the edge of downtown, which had plenty of alleys for losing cops. But no matter where I turned, the cops kept popping up. I was no expert getaway driver, but they really shouldn't have been able to follow me that well. Then I noticed a flashing radar icon on the scooter's view screen. It looked just like the Find My Device app on my phone. D'oh! They'd been tracking me all along.

I zipped behind a store called Breath of Fresh Heir, full of items with pictures of the royal children on them, and ditched the scooter there. Dashing away on foot, I turned a corner just as the cops pulled up. It was only a few blocks to the Janus, but everything seems far when you're wearing knickers and hose over jeans. A fresh coat of sweat covered me by the time I reached the hotel's employee entrance and slipped inside.

The empty hotel felt creepier than ever. Maybe that's because now I knew this wasn't just an old, abandoned hotel, but an old, abandoned hotel from another dimension. I rushed to the elevator bank and pressed the call button. The door couldn't have rattled open fast enough.

Right when I stepped inside, the cops reached the front entrance and pounded on the glass. Even without a code, they'd be inside in no time. I glanced over at the elevator control panel and realized with a wet-towel slap to my brain that I didn't know how to get back to my Earth. I'd never paid attention to the "floor" I'd left from. Which of these hundred buttons would take me there?

The entrance doors banged open and the cops burst in. Completely freaked, I pressed the first button handy: zero. It lit up like a green Christmas tree light.

Only after the elevator started moving did I remember the last origami note, the one that had told me to press zero in the first place.

That meant I was headed to Me Con, whether I liked it or not.

★ 12 ★

Me Con

You'd think piercing the barrier between realities in an elevator would be a bumpy ride, but the Janus elevator glided along like it was only going between floors, not whole dimensions. That didn't ease my nerves, not in the slightest. It had already been scary enough in this crate the first time around, and that was before I knew it could travel the multiverse.

I ditched the colonial outfit, but I couldn't shake the weirdness of walking around in the shoes of another Me. The wealth, the power, the smarts, the popularity. Were all Mes of other realities so irritatingly awesome? Hollywood wasn't—he was just irritating without the awesome. Still, hadn't he said something about acting on TV? I'd only met two copies of myself, and they'd both accomplished more than I or my Achieve-O-Meter could ever have dreamed. There was no telling what impressive stuff the other Mes at Me Con had done.

The elevator finally stopped, and the door opened on yet another Janus elevator bank. I faced a bench that hadn't been in the other two Janus Hotels. On its armrest sat a coffee mug with WORLD'S GREATEST FARTER on the side and blue bubbles shooting from the brim. I stepped out for a closer look. The foamy blue liquid inside fizzed like a potion in a mad scientist's lab. Who'd ever want to drink that? Then I noticed butt-cheek depressions in the cushion. Someone had just been here. A fellow Me?

I peered into the lobby but didn't see anybody, just a locked entrance and dark windows. Even though it should still have been daytime outside, the view was absolute black, as if the last shred of light had left and didn't plan on ever coming back. I couldn't tear my eyes away, until a noise snapped me out of it. The buzz of an electric motor.

I looked down the hall and saw a kid coming straight at me in a single-rider mobility cart. The Me behind the wheel was yet another version of me: same hair, same eyes, same age, same height. The only difference was his weight, an extra hundred pounds at least. He was large. Really large. The kind of large that needs a motorized cart to get around. It was like looking in a funhouse mirror and not being able to walk away.

Wheels whirring, engine buzzing, basket rattling, his cart got closer and closer. I tried to step back into the elevator, but the door had shut. All I could do now was stand there, frozen, as he pulled up to me.

He held out a meaty hand. "Sorry I'm late." He sounded more like me than Meticulous or Hollywood had. No accent, no attitude. "Don't worry. We may be interdimensional doppelgängers, but we won't explode on contact or anything. Welcome to Me Con."

★ 13 ★

More of Me

My latest double shook hands the way I did—limp and floppy. He chewed on his lower lip like me too, and slouched the same way. He was like a living, breathing reminder of all my bad habits. Plus, he was huge. I'd like to think I wouldn't judge somebody for their size, but since he looked like me in every other way, I couldn't stop staring. How did somebody so much like me end up with a body so different from mine?

His cheeks spread into a grin that looked familiar, despite the extra padding. "This is the part where you're supposed to say, 'Interdimensional doppelgänger? What are you talking about?'"

I shrugged, hoping my shoulders weren't shaking too

much. "No, I pretty much get it. Parallel worlds and all that." I shot a glance down the hall, just in case Meticulous or Hollywood was lurking there.

The Me looked impressed. "Well, that's a first. Normally I have to talk new Mes off the wall. But I can tell you're playing it cool. I try to play it cool the same way, you know."

He hardened his jaw and scrunched his eyebrows. I felt my skin flame up. I'd been making that exact face.

He laughed a deep belly laugh, the way I laughed, just with more belly. "Lighten up. I'm only joking."

This was getting more awkward by the second, so I changed the subject. "How did you even know I was coming here?"

"The SecureMe cam in the elevator lobby. I'm on Welcome Committee duty. Can't believe I get to meet the Me from Earth Ninety-Nine. That's the last Earth the elevator can reach, you know. Feels like the end of an era. By the way, call me Motor Me."

"Motor Me?"

"Yeah, every Me at Me Con needs one."

"Every Me needs a mobility cart?!"

His face went a shade of red that probably matched mine. Great, now I'd gone and insulted myself.

"Every Me needs a nickname, is what I meant," he mumbled. "They're how we tell each other apart, since we're all Meade Macon. By the way, the other Mes aren't plus-size like me. I'm a special case." He pulled out a tube of cookies. "And on that note, want some?"

The package read CHEMICALLY FLAVORED CRUNCHIES.

"Weird name for a cookie," I said.

"Oh, that." Motor opened the pack, and the smell of artificial figs filled the air. "Marketing is a little different on my world. Companies use honest names. It's the law or something."

"'Chemically Flavored' doesn't exactly make me hungry."

Motor offered me the tube. "Never stopped me."

Keeping an eye out for any sudden moves, I took a cookie. It looked like an Oreo, but with gooey fig filling inside instead of cream. "I've never seen a cookie like this."

"I always pack a few things I can only get at home."

I twisted apart the top and bottom wafers to scrape up the filling with my teeth. It wasn't bad at all.

Motor clapped his hands together. "That's how I eat them too!"

Maybe it was just the sugar talking, but this kid's goofy good cheer was starting to rub off on me. "Duh! Didn't you say you're me?"

He laughed. "Differences do crop up. Like eating habits. The other Mes just bite into them whole, and only one at a time."

"Boring."

"I know, right? Why stop at just one?" Motor stacked three cookies atop each other and opened wide, sinking his teeth into the cookie sandwich with crumb-spraying bliss. He waggled his eyebrows as if to say, *Top that.*

With no hesitation, I grabbed the last five Chemically Flavored Crunchies from the tube, gripped them lengthwise between my thumb and forefinger, and took a huge chomp from the middle. The chain of cookies held together.

Motor's jaw dropped. "I've always tried to do that, but it's never worked!"

I did my gruff-old-coach impersonation. "Just the right amount of pressure and slack in the fingers, that's the key."

"That's Tom Furst you're doing, isn't it?! The dude who ran the tennis camp? I haven't thought about him for years!"

"You knew him?" Here was one good thing about Me Con already: an audience that got my most obscure references.

"Of course! Mom and Dad forced tennis lessons on me too."

The thought of Mom and Dad—my real mom and dad—stabbed me with guilt. After-school basketball and theater practice would be wrapping up soon, and they'd expect me home for dinner. They'd freak when I didn't show.

Motor glanced at a MeMinder on his lumpy wrist. "I came here to give you the standard meet and greet, but right now the opening party's wrapping up and it's every Me for himself when it comes to the cake. Grandma Sue's recipe. You know the one."

"German chocolate." My mouth watered a little.

Motor launched the cart back in the direction he'd come

from. "You can follow me or go back to your Earth. Either way, thanks for showing me the cookie trick."

Swallowing the last of the fig goo in my mouth, I watched him leave. I wondered what to do next. Just because I shared a face and some memories with Motor didn't mean I could trust him. Plus, I didn't know what waited for me in that ballroom. On top of everything else, I'd eventually get ratted out by Hollywood once he came here.

Still, how would he and Meticulous know it was me? This sounded like the sort of crowd I could blend into, and Motor seemed like a decent guy. How could a person who ate cookies with so much gusto be all that bad? If other Mes were more like Motor and less like Meticulous and Hollywood, maybe this Me Con thing would be okay. Besides, I'd come all this way.

What was the harm in a quick peek?

★ 14 ★

The Multiverse According to Me

When I caught up with Motor, he smiled around a mouthful of chips called Sodium Headachies. "Other Mes usually take longer to decide," he said. "You'd be surprised how many nearly end up going back."

"But they all stick around in the end?"

Motor cleared his throat the way I did when somebody asked me a question I didn't want to answer. "Well, we've lost a few since the first Me Con."

"The first Me Con? How long has this thing been going on?"

"Some of us from the low-numbered Earths got the invite when we were ten. We've been meeting every other month ever since."

My mind would have been even more blown by all this at age ten. I had about a zillion other questions, but I settled for "So what universe are you from?"

Motor stopped his cart again and pulled out a lanyard hidden in the folds of his shirt. A laminated name tag dangled from the end: MOTOR ME. EARTH ELEVEN.

"And I'm from Earth Ninety-Nine? Is it really the last Earth out there?"

Motor snorted. Did my snorts sound so . . . snorty? "You didn't pay much attention to Mom's lectures, did you? Don't worry, neither did I, not until I came here. The Earths the elevator can reach are just a small sliver of what's out there. The truth is, there's no end to them."

"How's that possible?"

"Scads of new universes get birthed every second of the day." He held up the bag of Sodium Headachies and scooped a handful into his mouth. "We decide to eat these and BAM! That's a universe." He held up a chocolate bar labeled THE BOWEL BLOCKER. "We go with this instead and BAM! That's another universe." He tore open the packet and ate the bar whole.

"And if you choose to eat both, what does that make?"

Motor waved at his belly with the drama of a stage magician. "A very fat Me."

The joke seemed forced, and I forced a smile in return. It's not always easy to laugh at yourself.

"So you're saying there's just one Sodium Headachie of a difference between Earth One and Earth Two?" I said.

"There's no rhyme or reason to the Earths the elevator can access. It's a random selection, near as I can tell. Some of the Mes at Me Con come from Earths that split off from each other way before we were born. Like on Earth Sixty-Six, where Escape Me comes from, the Belgians were the ones who built the ancient pyramids. Surely you've heard of the Great Pyramid of Antwerp?"

"So what did the Egyptians do? Invent Belgian waffles?"

Motor laughed. "Aside from little details like that, most of us come from pretty similar Earths. I mean, sure, the Roman Empire never fell on the Earths where the Toga Mes come from, and the Old West stayed wild where Cowboy Me hangs his ten-gallon hat or whatever, but those differences haven't changed their worlds as much as you'd think. Technology developed about the same, give or take a self-driving car here or a holographic projector there. It's actually a little boring sometimes. I'd kill to meet a Me from an Earth where they're still cave dwellers, or magic is real. You know, really far-out stuff."

"You're bored with Me Con? I'm still on the verge of a heart attack just from the elevator ride to get here."

Motor gave me a thoughtful look. "You're actually taking this really well. Most new Mes are too freaked out to even ask where the bathroom is."

We passed some graffiti scrawled on the wall. It was written in my—our—handwriting: A*LL* O*F* M*E* W*ILL* R*ETURN*!

"All of Me?" I asked.

Motor scoffed. "It's just a dumb legend. All of Me is a

mythical figure at Me Con who some Mes believe in. Supposedly, he can do anything that any Me can do. The legend says he'll 'save every Me in our greatest hour of need.'"

"Is that a joke?"

He shrugged. "To most Mes it is. Some take it kinda seriously."

"How about you?"

Motor looked surprised, like he wasn't used to someone caring what he thought. But before he could answer, speakers in the ballroom up ahead started blasting music. I could just make out people moving around.

"Dang it!" said Motor. "The music's already started! That means we missed the cake!"

Thinking about a room full of Mes stopped me cold.

Motor rolled his cart up beside me. "It's weird, but you get used to it."

"But what if—"

"What if they don't like you? What if you're not as good as them? What if they reject you?"

"Yeah."

"Take my advice and be yourself."

He was just as bad as me at trying to sell a lie.

★ 15 ★

More of Me to Go Around

Stepping into the Janus ballroom and its wall-to-wall Mes was like being blasted with every embarrassing photo and video of myself a zillion times over. Was that how I walked? Was that what my neck hair looked like? Did my nose really make that noise when I sneezed?

What must have been a hundred Mes either stood around in clumps or sat together at tables. The curved walls and tiled floor of the ballroom bounced their voices—my voice, I should say—back to me over and over. I'd never felt so self-conscious.

"Just focus on how they're different from you, not the same," said Motor, reading my mind. "It's less weird that way."

He was right. The Mes might have looked and sounded just like me, but at the same time, they were nothing like me at all. They had different hairstyles, clothes, and glasses. Some stood up straight; some slouched. Some Mes even had muscles, which they flexed as much as possible.

Motor watched me gawping at them and chuckled. "Yeah, the Fit Mes do stand out."

"Fit Mes?"

"This place is kind of like a school—everybody's in a clique, but the cliques are different variations of the same person. The Play Mes, for instance." He pointed to a cluster of Mes at a table, dealing cards in an intense round of a game from another Earth called Magic: The Blathering, which seemed to involve a lot more talking than Magic: The Gathering did. Pasty-skinned and frail, they looked like a Me after a few weeks in a food dehydrator.

We passed a pack of puffed-up Mes in clothes my parents could never have afforded. "The Money Mes," Motor whispered. "Mom and Dad struck it rich on their Earths."

Nearby, a group of shaggy Mes played Hacky Sack ("Chill Mes") next to Mes wearing dress shirts and ties and making spreadsheets and PowerPoint presentations on their laptops ("Work Mes").

"How could these guys possibly be me?" I said. "I have nothing in common with them."

"It's all perception. If you're a Fit Me who sticks with other Fit Mes all the time, of course you're gonna think you have nothing in common with the Alterna Mes." He pointed to some sullen Mes in the corner with creative hairstyles and black clothing.

I definitely didn't see anything I had in common with the pack of Mes dressed like clowns, mimes, and stand-up comics from the nineties. They practiced walking up and down invisible stairs and doing ventriloquism using each other as dummies. "The Silly Mes," Motor said with a shudder.

As we passed more Mes, some nodded at us, a few smiled, but nobody actually said hi. What had I been expecting, some sort of hero's welcome? *Look, everyone, a new brother has arrived! Hurray!* I was nothing but another Me in this crowd, and a pretty pathetic one at that.

More than a few Mes smirked at the sight of Motor, and I got the impression he was a joke around here. The idea of Mes laughing at other Mes behind their own backs seemed both sad and completely bizarre.

"So what exactly made everybody turn out different?" I said. "Aren't we all supposed to be the same?"

"Sure, but our worlds aren't. A little variation in any given environment can tweak DNA, and it just takes a tweak for a Me to turn out big or scrawny, arty or science-y. And after that, nurture takes over. The Fit Mes stay in shape by playing sports or whatever all the time. The Play Mes hone their gaming skills through constant practice."

"But what makes them want to devote all that energy to sports training or game playing or whatever they're into?" I tried not to sound too desperate, but I had to know how we Mes actually got good at something.

Motor gestured toward the stage, where four Mes bickered with each other while setting up their guitars and drums and turntables. "Take them, the Tune Mes, the musicians of Me Con. They don't actually play when they get together—too busy arguing about who gets the first solo and stuff like that. How do you think they're different from the Fit Mes?"

"I don't know. Music in their DNA?"

"Yeah, but another thing too: Weezer."

"You mean that old band Dad's always going on about?"

"The same. Except they got to go to the Weezer concert when they were nine."

"Really? Dad got sick and couldn't take me. He was so bummed."

"Dad got sick on my Earth too." A cloud passed over his face, but it lifted once he stuffed his mouth with a handful of Cavity Pellets. "The Tune Mes got to go, and the show was so good it inspired them to take up music."

"So that's all it takes? A couple of genes and a concert?"

"No, but it's those pivotal moments that pushed us in different directions. Plenty of Mes who wound up seeing Weezer never got into music. But they got exposed to other, totally different things that shaped them instead." He nodded toward a bunch of decidedly less cool Mes practicing some dorky Broadway musical routine. "Take the Look at Mes, the actors of Me Con. Grandma Sue played them the soundtrack to *Brigadoon* every day in the car during that week we spent with her the summer after first grade."

"Ugh! She did that to me too. Seven days of 'Down on MacConnachy Square.' Scarred me for life."

Motor chortled. "Me too! But they liked it."

I felt a pang of jealousy toward these talented Mes. Whether it was soccer, drums, computer programming, or whatever, my laziness and general incompetence had kept me from sticking with anything. I'd barely dabbled in stuff they'd completely mastered. Even among my different selves, I was a nobody.

The MeMinder naturally chose this moment to announce, "Science fair project not yet complete. Student Showcase tonight."

Motor chuckled and raised his own MeMinder, a more advanced model than mine. "If you want it to shut up, just reset it."

"Why didn't I think of that?!"

He grinned. "Sometimes two Mes are better than one."

In a weird way, that made me feel better.

Motor and I moved past a long line of Mes waiting outside a door guarded by an impossibly huge Me. He wore a black suit with white pinstripes, a fedora to match, and black-and-white dress shoes.

"What's that thing?!" I asked.

Motor groaned. "Mobster Me. He does security."

"He's a mobster?!"

"I guess. Or everybody on his Earth dresses like that all the time. He doesn't talk much, so nobody knows."

"What's he guarding?"

"The Viral Me Lounge." Motor ripped open a bag of Diarrhea Delights. "They're Mes who think they've done something important just because they've gotten some notice on the internet or TV. They're so 'famous' they worry they'd get mobbed if they didn't have their own private hangout. As if."

"But isn't Me Con supposed to be about everybody sharing and talking and stuff?"

"Tell me about it." Motor tossed me two bags of Diarrhea Delights. "These have pomegranate in them. You're not allergic, are you? Some Mes are."

I didn't care to find out, so I shoved the bags into my pocket. "Thanks."

The crowd parted for a pack of four Mes who strutted out of the lounge like they owned the place. The Me at the front of the group wore leather armor with a thick chain mail belt and a long mane of hair that made him look like an extra from *Game of Thrones*.

"Is his Earth stuck in the Middle Ages?" I asked.

Motor scrunched his nose like he smelled something stinky. "Ren Faire Me? He claims his Earth 'clings to the old ways.' But then, he claims a lot of things, including that he's the most

84

famous actor on his world. All I know for sure is he's a real jerk."

"What about the ones with him?"

"The skinny one is Click Me. He's built a huge audience making those kinds of internet videos that sound cool at first but turn out to be completely stupid and boring, like opening product packaging to see what's inside. The one with the arm cast is Dare Me. He does idiotic stunts on camera, like jumping off roofs or getting bitten by bugs on purpose."

"I'm so glad I've never tried to go viral."

The Me who followed behind them looked like he hadn't bothered to take off his mask after Halloween. His nose had the shape of a stress ball stuck in midsqueeze, and his overbite would have made him right at home on *The Simpsons*. But all I could focus on was his ears.

"They're . . . pointy?!"

Motor made a barf face. "That's Troll Me. He insists the ears are real, that everybody on his Earth has them. But he's not exactly a trustworthy kind of guy, so he's more than likely just messing with us. As for the nose, I'm convinced he gets punched in the face a lot back home for being a jerk."

"What's he done to go viral?"

"When he's not busy trolling people, he posts videos of

himself hacking video games. People will watch anything, I guess."

"And these are the most famous Mes?"

"Well, there's Hollywood Me. He started the Viral Me Lounge. But he hasn't been around for a while. My theory is he collapsed under the weight of his own ego."

I faked a chuckle to mask my panic. It was only a matter of time before Hollywood escaped from the limo on Earth One, made his way to Me Con, and ratted me out.

"What's wrong?" asked Motor.

"Nothing. So how do you know so much about all these Mes?"

Motor gulped down a handful of Diarrhea Delights. "Panel discussions. Every Me shares his story at some point. So will you. It's sort of mandatory."

"What if I don't have anything worthwhile to tell?"

"You'll think of something. Which reminds me, you need to do your interview."

"Interview?"

"To find out what you're good at so you can talk about it in panels."

"I don't like the sound of that."

"It's mostly a quick checklist you'll go over when you register with the Me who runs this whole shebang."

"And what Me is that again?"

"He's over this way." Motor led me past another row of darkened windows toward a table in the far corner of the room. The sign above it read REGISTRATION AND PROGRAMMING.

A Me was just sitting down at the table as we approached, a Me I recognized in an instant.

That tidy hair, that perfect posture, that pressed suit . . . that pressed *colonial*-style suit.

Meticulous Me.

The Me who ran Me Con was the same Me whose life I'd just stolen.

Somehow, I doubted he'd be thrilled about that.

★ 16 ★

A Brand-New Me

Meticulous Me waved me over like a king ready to receive his next audience. Motor practically had to prod me forward with his cart. "It's just an interview. Nothing to worry about."

Yeah, just an interview with an impossibly powerful guy I'd impersonated on his home turf. Me Con probably had rules about stealing another Me's life, and I'd broken all of them.

"Look, it's a brand-new Me," Motor told Meticulous when we finally reached the table.

Meticulous rolled his eyes at what had to be a tired joke among Mes. "Thanks, mate." He pulled a handful of pens from his bag and lined them up on the table just so. "That'll be all. I believe you have a panel to moderate in a few minutes?"

Motor gave me an encouraging wink and rolled away.

Meticulous was all business as he pulled out a pristine MePad and tapped at the screen. "So, you're the Me from Earth Ninety-Nine, the last stop on the elevator." He sounded annoyed as he said this, like it was my fault the elevator couldn't go higher. "Welcome to Me Con. I see you got my invites."

"Yeah." Out of nerves, I pulled a bag of Diarrhea Delights from my pocket and ripped it open. Then I remembered I didn't even like fruit-flavored candy, so I let it sit there in front of me.

Meticulous rubbed imaginary dirt off his fingers as he eyed the screen. "Have you been having a good time so far?"

I didn't hear any edge to the words, no hint that he was about to scream at me. Mostly he just seemed bored. Maybe he didn't know the truth after all.

"Sure, it's great here."

"Brilliant. Well, I have a few details for us to go over. Do you have any medical conditions we should know about? Cancer? Heart problems?"

"No. But do other Mes?"

He ignored the question as he tapped a check on the screen. "How about allergies?"

"No."

"Romantic status?"

"There's a romantic status?"

"I'm going to mark no."

"Right."

"What about injuries? How did you come out after the little row with the three-legged dog in third grade?"

"You mean Roscoe from a few houses up?" I cringed at the memory. I should never have cut across the Mullinses' lawn that time. "Yeah, he bit me. In the ankle. No rabies, though."

"Has Nash ever sent you to the hospital?"

"No. The way he bullies me is—"

"Psychological. The 'nice bully' routine. Quite. I'm familiar with that one." For just a second, he stared off into space, a haunted look in his eyes. Clearly, his Nash had left some scars before he started sucking up to Meticulous.

"So, about Mum and Dad on your world," Meticulous continued, back to business. "How's the company doing?"

"Me Co.? Never took off. It's more of a side project."

"Interesting." Meticulous sounded anything but interested. "Tell me, are they still together?"

His words didn't register at first. "Uh, together?"

He patted his tidy hair into an even tidier shape. "Are they divorced? Sixty percent of Mums and Dads out there have split."

Divorced. It was like he'd slapped me in the face with the word. I hadn't ever thought Mom and Dad might break up, but maybe I'd just been avoiding the idea. They definitely fought like a couple on the verge of calling it quits.

"They're still together." Then I blurted, "And Mom's alive."

Meticulous's eyes bored into me. "Why would you say that? Is she in bad health?" In a blink he'd gone from big-shot CEO to anxious thirteen-year-old kid. It was like watching a wolfman turn back into a naked guy. I could see by the pain on his face that his mom's death still hurt.

"Uh, she's fine," I said. "I just thought I should bring this up in case she—or Dad—is dead on other Earths."

Meticulous pulled himself together enough to glower at me. "Kind of a morbid thought, don't you think, mate?"

"Call me Morbid Me, I guess. Heh."

Meticulous straightened up and adjusted his cravat. Back to business. He glanced at the MePad. "And that brings us to technology. Based on that very primitive MeMinder on your wrist, and from what I saw when I paid you a visit, I'm guessing your Earth is still working on self-driving cars, personalized drone deliveries, and interactive public loos."

I recovered just enough to fake a laugh. "Interactive public loos? Who ever heard of such a thing? You'd never catch me using one of those!"

"Indeed." He seemed disappointed, but at least he wasn't suspicious. "Okay, nearly done. How about sports? Football? Cricket? Conkers?"

"Just basketball, sort of. Not much of an athlete."

Meticulous looked me up and down. "I gathered as much. What about creative endeavors? Music? Painting? Writing?"

I scanned the room. The Tune Mes had stormed off after their argument, so the Silly Mes had taken the stage, miming a tug-of-war with an invisible rope. By the water fountain, Kabuki Theater Me did an elaborate dance with a foldable hand fan. Nearby, Cowboy Me performed lasso tricks. Across from him, Escape Me thrilled a crowd by picking the lock on the chains that held him suspended over a tank of water.

Compared to them, I felt more than a little worthless. It was like I'd lost a contest with myself. As if to rub it in, the MeMinder piped up: "Science fair project remains incomplete. Basketball practice unattended. You are unprepared for upcoming Student Showcase."

Meticulous snorted, but in a much meaner way than Motor.

"I can't do anything special," I grumbled. "Beyond origami, I guess."

Meticulous's eyes went wide. He recovered the next second, back to playing it cool. "So, what, you can fold some flowers? Maybe a crane?"

Glad for the chance to show up this guy, I took a blank sheet of paper from the pile on the table and folded it into an octopus. My best octopus, the three-dimensional one with a balloon head, a dagger beak, and rows of suckers on the arms. When I plopped the finished product in front of Meticulous, he flinched like the creature might come to life and latch on to his face.

I milked the moment for all it was worth. "Aren't other

Mes into origami too? Since you folded those notes for me, I just assumed it came naturally to all of us."

Meticulous licked his lips. Did I lick my lips? "Can you fold other things?"

"Sure."

Meticulous rustled around in his bag. "Will you do some origami for me? I've been trying to teach myself, but it's slow going."

"Uh, okay." Maybe doing him a favor now would help smooth things over if he ever found out about my little visit to his Earth.

Meticulous placed a SecureMe camera-projector on the desk, just like the one I'd seen on his world. At the sight of it, the stolen flash drive burned in my pocket. "And mind if I holo-record this? If I can watch it on the replay, that would help my technique."

He pressed a button on the box, and the lens lit up, beaming a green light that formed into a piece of holo-paper. "Just fold it like you would normal paper."

"Cool. So how do I start?"

Meticulous sighed. "Grab the holo-paper and start folding, obviously." He called up a file on his MePad and glanced at it. "Can you start with a Lahontan cutthroat trout? I know it's an odd choice, but—"

"Nah, it's cool. I know my way around a Lahontan cutthroat trout."

"Really?"

"I've done plenty."

The hologram felt like real paper at my touch, bending and creasing with ease. Still, I couldn't quite get the hang of folding in midair.

Meticulous scoffed. "Just lay it flat!"

I tugged on the holo-paper and it lay flat on the desk, ready for folding. In just a few seconds I turned it into a fish. I could tell Meticulous was impressed but trying not to show it.

The trout disappeared in a silent burst, and a new, blank sheet of paper blinked in its place.

Meticulous glanced at his notes. "Next on my list is a moustached puffbird, but I'm sure you can't handle that, so we can move on."

"No, I've done a moustached puffbird before." I folded one in a matter of seconds.

Once Meticulous gave it a reluctant thumbs-up, the bird popped out of existence and a new sheet appeared.

"Next up, a yellow-bellied sapsucker."

It went on like this. Paper in, naked mole rat out. Paper in, blobfish out. It was actually a little odd how familiar I was with all the animals he named, like I'd gotten hold of the answers before the test. But the best part was showing up Meticulous. He looked more and more baffled with every origami I made.

Finally, after I put the last touches on a Japanese spider crab, Meticulous turned off the recorder.

"That'll do, mate." His voice had gone flat. "Just what I need."

He tapped the screen, and a printer at his side spewed out a card that he tossed to me: AVERAGE ME, EARTH NINETY-NINE.

"Average Me?"

"Your interview results show that you fall in the perfect average of every Me benchmark."

What did it say about me that *average* was my defining trait? To wear that on a name tag would spell my doom at Me Con. Who'd want to hang out with Average Me? It was like wearing a cone of shame. Now everybody would know I hadn't accomplished jack with my life.

"But what about, I don't know, Origami Me? Wouldn't that be a better nickname?"

Meticulous tapped the MePad screen, and the printer spat out more paper. "Your origami's cracking, but not cracking enough to merit a nickname. Don't worry about it. Just enjoy yourself here. The panels, the games, the parties. We're chockablock with fun. That's what Me Con is all about. I've given you some right proper panels to speak on, if that makes you feel better."

He handed me the paper from the printer, a list titled *Average Me's Panels.* He'd scheduled me to speak on "Bedtime Blues Part Seven: The Recurring Evil Otter Boot Camp Nightmare" and "Barfing in Burger King: Our Most Outrageous Episodes of Public Puking."

"Have fun." Meticulous slipped the holo-recorder and other stuff into his bag.

I stood up, eager to get out while the getting was good.

But then a blur of green ran up to the table. Hollywood was back, his colonial suit all ripped and rumpled. He hunched over to catch his breath.

Meticulous scowled at him. "Some bloody assistant you turned out to be! I couldn't find you anywhere! Had to leave without you!"

Hollywood gulped some air and stood up. "I had to bust out of your limo! Didn't you hear me screaming?!"

"That was you? I thought it was a squeaky brake."

Looking hurt by this, Hollywood pointed at me. "He trapped me in the fudging boot, if you'll excuse my colorful language! This Me broke into your world somehow! He took your trophy at the science fair! He sat in your office! He escaped on your scooter!"

Meticulous's lips parted with the precision of a C-clamp. "How did you get to my world!?"

"Uh, I pressed the number one on the elevator?"

Meticulous pounded his fist on the table so hard my bag of Diarrhea Delights slid to the edge. Hollywood picked it up and shoved a handful into his mouth.

"Mes can only go to two bloody places on the elevator: Me Con and their home world!" said Meticulous. "I programmed it that way!"

At this point, I was too mad to let this pompous jerk scare me anymore. "Why do we only get to visit one stop, while you go wherever you want?! Who are you to control where we can and can't go?!"

The Mes nearby stopped what they were doing and

turned to us. Meticulous lowered his voice to a hiss. "I built the elevator! I started Me Con! And I set up the rules to keep everyone safe! That means nobody gets to world-jump but me! It's too bloody dodgy!"

Mobster and Ren Faire crossed the room and stood on either side of Meticulous, squeezing their fists and cracking their necks in menacing ways. Trying to look just as

tough, Hollywood stood in front of them and folded his arms over his chest. He came across more stupid than scary. Meticulous noticed him and shook his head in disgust. "You've made a right botch of this, Hollywood! You're in trouble too!"

"Me?! Why?!"

"Because thou art a half-wit!" said Ren Faire. "Leave it to a TV actor to bungle a job so simple!"

"Hollywood," said Meticulous, "from this point forward, I revoke your elevator privileges. From now on you can only go to your Earth and Me Con, and that's it. Oh, and you're on waiter duty too."

Hollywood started to cry, which was just as embarrassing to watch as if I'd cried myself. "Geez Louise! Anything but that!"

Meticulous stood up. "I'd better go home and fix whatever damage this wally has done. Mobster, Ren Faire, take him to the Exit."

The growing crowd of Mes around us made a collective gasp of surprise. Apparently, the Exit wasn't good. But my brain barely registered this as Ren Faire and Mobster stepped forward and snatched me by the wrists.

That's when the fizz came back. Just like before, a feeling of strength and speed spread over my arms and legs. With that surge of something—adrenaline? sugar rush?— I broke free of Ren Faire and Mobster. They even staggered back a few steps.

Meticulous barked a laugh. "You can't possibly think you can fight those two!"

Ren Faire drew his sword as Mobster put on a set of brass knuckles.

"Who said anything about fighting?" And before anybody could grab me again, I turned in the opposite direction and ran.

★ 17 ★

Oh Me Oh My

I darted through the crowd of confused Mes and ducked into the nearest hallway, slipping into a panel called "Surprise Me: The Little Differences Between Our Worlds." Nobody in the room had seen me escape from Ren Faire and Mobster, so I kept my head low and took the last seat available in the back. I sat next to a Me in a leather jacket with his hair greased back, a classic 1950s rebel-without-a-cause type. JUVENILE HALL ME, read his name tag. He even had an old-timey slingshot sticking out of his back pocket, though that didn't look nearly as dangerous as the switchblade he flipped over and over in his hand. I gulped.

Glancing around to make sure I hadn't been followed, I tried to round up my racing thoughts. One thing was clear:

Me Con was more dangerous than I'd ever imagined. I needed to get to the elevator and back to my world. But that would mean going through the ballroom again and straight into the hands of Ren Faire and Mobster. For now at least, I was stuck.

Motor's voice came over the room speaker: "So let's get this part out of the way." He sat at the table up front with three other Mes. "What's *that* certain beloved sci-fi movie series called on your Earths? I think we all know what I'm talking about!"

"You mean *Space Wars*?" said the Me on Motor's right side. He wore brass-plated goggles, a top hat, and a pirate shirt with a ruffled front. His name tag read Steampunk Me.

"No, he means *Laser Sword Warriors in Spaceships*!" said a Me in an army-style uniform on Motor's left. Military School Me, read his name tag.

"Who cares?" said a crabby Me at the far end of the table. I recognized him from earlier: Troll Me, one of the Virals. He focused on the MePad in his hands, like he had more important things to do than join in this discussion.

"On my Earth it's called *Star Wars: Bad Guy Is Good Guy's Dad*," said Motor. "We have a thing about honest titles where I'm from, and nobody cares if they're spoilers. You know, like *Titanic: The Ship Sinks.*"

"That's stupid!" said Troll.

Motor frowned but said nothing. He wouldn't even look Troll in the eyes.

Steampunk tried to steer the talk to safer ground. "Motor, if everything's honest on your Earth, what do they call the first Harry Potter book?"

Motor shrugged. *Harry Potter and the Bad Guy Who Stuck Himself on Another Guy's Head.*"

That cracked everybody up except Troll. "Idiotic!" he yelled.

Awkward silence followed as Motor stared at the floor. Finally, Military School told the crowd that nobody on his Earth had ever invented handfarting, Velcro shoes, or tetherball. Steampunk explained that his Earth treated corn dogs and funnel cake as high cuisine and punished the crime of gleeking on another person with jail time. Troll shared nothing beyond his bad attitude, grumbling to himself and tapping at his screen. When Motor mentioned that shadow puppetry was one of the most venerated art forms on his Earth, Troll was at his throat again. "That explains everything! If you come from an Earth that dumb, you must be dumb too! You couldn't hack your way out of an Atari 2600!"

Troll kept laying into him, and Motor kept on taking it. Meanwhile, none of the Mes on the panel or in the audience spoke out to defend him. Some even chuckled, probably to get in good with Troll. I couldn't believe all these Mes would just sit there and let this bully get away with it. "Why isn't anybody saying anything?" I asked no one in particular.

Juvenile Hall ran a comb through his greased hair in a luxurious sweep. "Troll's a Viral Me, you dig? Nobody speaks out against Viral Mes, daddy-o. Plus, it's only Motor Me he's dissing. Who cares about that cat?"

Motor was on the verge of tears. If he cried in front of everybody, he'd never live this down. I'd meant to lie low, but I couldn't watch another second of this. I grabbed a couple of leftover Diarrhea Delights from my pocket and yanked the slingshot out of Juvenile Hall's pocket.

"Slow down, Jack!" said Juvenile Hall. "What gives?!"

Ignoring him, I shoved a few of the chocolate lumps into the sling and lined up the shot. Though I'd never used one of these things before, I just knew I could make the target. Maybe it had something to do with the return of the fizz. I felt it in my eyes and hands this time, making my vision clear and my grip steady. I stretched the strap and let loose, pegging Troll square in the forehead. Chocolate, caramel, and pomegranate splattered his face.

Troll stood up and screamed, "Who did this?" All he got in reply was everybody's laughter. Real laughter this time, not the brown-nosing kind.

Juvenile Hall slapped me on the back. "What a shot! You're wild, man! As in ferocious wild! A Wild Me!"

"Uh, thanks." I tossed the slingshot back to him. "Better hide this. That little weasel's on the warpath."

Troll got so shouty that his pointy ears wiggled. Monk Me—a Me with a shaved head and orange robes—jumped up from the audience and demanded that everybody do stress-reducing yoga moves. This struck me as a good time to slip away.

I'd just tiptoed through the back exit when Ren Faire and Mobster kicked open the main doors and rushed in. They both pointed at me, shouting in unison: "You!" That startled Monk Me so much he bonked his head during a special pose from his Earth called Poop-Hurling Chimpanzee.

As I hustled out of there, I glanced at Motor. He mouthed two words to me: "Ice machine." Whatever that meant.

I stumbled into the adjoining room, which had been dimmed for a slide show: "Where's Mr. Fartz? The Final Fate of Our Beloved Toys." In the dark, I snuck past other Mes, who were too busy weeping to notice me passing through. No sooner had I slipped into "The Lunt Conspiracy: Why He Hates Us" than Ren Faire and Mobster followed right behind. Troll, still huffing mad, tagged along with them. They kept on my tail as I sprinted through "No More Nash: Humiliate Him Without Getting Caught!" and "Twig: From

Friend to Girlfriend—but Don't Hold Your Breath."

I didn't lose them until I reached "Challenge Me: The Ultimate in Self-Competition," where I hid under a VR helmet to compete in the Battle Royale Edition of *Brawl of Duty: Battle of the Mall of America.* After losing to a group of Play Mes in all of two minutes, I moved on to a self-help workshop nearby called "Trust Me: Gettin' in Touch with Yourself." I might have stayed, but a nearby homework swap called "It's Not Cheating If a Me Did It" sounded too tempting. I went there looking for a ready-made science fair project but found the Virals waiting for me instead.

They chased me into a little-used section of the hotel with no panels or other Mes in sight, just more of those weird, lightless windows with nothing but blackness on the other side. I got lost in a maze of halls where the carpet had gone ragged and the walls needed new paint. Barely keeping one step ahead of the goons, I hopped into an old abandoned laundry cart just as Mobster's deep voice boomed from around the corner. "Wish we could catch that dirty rat already so we can get outta here!"

The Virals passed nail-bitingly close to the cart, near enough to look inside if they had the notion.

"Patience, good sir," said Ren Faire.

"Mobster's got a point, though," said Troll. "It won't be long before Meticulous puts the plan in motion. I for one don't want to be stuck here when that happens."

104

"That shan't be us, I can assure you," said Ren Faire. "Not if we perform our endeavor with cunning and diligence."

They moved down the hall without noticing me, and after a few minutes I felt safe enough to climb out. I was glad to escape those psychos, but part of me wanted to follow them just so I could eavesdrop a little more. What was this plan they were talking about?

Before I could decide which way to go next, I heard muffled Me voices coming from the room on my left. A sign on the closed door read Ice Machine Room. This was the place Motor wanted me to go! The doorknob wouldn't budge, so I knocked. Everyone inside went whispery. After a long pause the door creaked open and a Me poked his head around. It was Steampunk Me, from Motor's panel. "Sorry, no official con event here. This is just a little, uh, social meeting."

"Could you sound any more suspicious?" said another Me behind him. "Let him in. I know this guy."

Grumbling to himself, Steampunk opened the door wide.

I stepped into a teeny room stuffed with an ice machine and a handful of Mes on metal folding chairs.

Plus one in a mobility cart.

Motor gave me a little wave. "Hey, Average. Welcome to the Why Mes."

★ 18 ★

The Why Mes

I almost cried out in relief at the sight of Motor, but he gave me a look that said, *Play it cool.*

Motor waved me to a seat next to Monk Me. "It's okay. I can vouch for Average Me."

Nobody objected when I sat down. Apparently, they didn't know I was on the run.

"So, my brothers, as I was saying," said Monk, "Meticulous may have created the elevator, but we can use it for so much more than Me Con. Like spreading a spirit of peace and inner calm through all dimensions. And while we're at it, spreading my music through all dimensions too. I've got a very positive, mind-expanding message that people on other Earths need to hear."

The twitchy Me next to him darted his eyes around the room, nervous. He'd either drunk too much caffeine or been possessed by the spirit of a squirrel. His name tag read ALIEN ABDUCTION ME. "What we need to do is use the elevator for hunting down the aliens who experimented on me! Area Fifty-One! Crop circles! The Knights Templar! It's all a big cover-up! We can expose it!"

Monk looked concerned. "My brother, how many times do I have to tell you? It's all in your head. You weren't abducted by aliens any more than Steampunk comes from an actual steampunk world."

Steampunk's top hat wobbled as he shook with rage. "I do so come from a steampunk world! Why does no one believe that?!"

"I mean no disrespect, my brother," said Monk. "But there comes a time when every Me must face the truth."

"I'm not lying! I come from a steampunk world! I'd take you there if I could!"

"Real or no, you've put together a nice costume," said Motor. "We can all agree on that."

Steampunk pouted and crossed his arms, his clockwork gear cuff links clinking together.

Alien Abduction shook his head, eyes bugging out. "I'm

telling you, the aliens will be back for me! For all of us! The government is in on it!"

Monk patted him on the shoulder, murmuring comforting words. "Those aliens you imagined aren't real. They don't have green skin and forehead antennae. It's all in your head. There, there."

"So, is this a counseling group or something?" I asked.

"Half the time it feels more like the Let's Make Fun of Steampunk Me Society," said Steampunk.

"We talk about stuff that otherwise doesn't come up a lot at Me Con," Motor said around the handful of Sodium Headachies he'd crammed into his mouth. "Stuff that Meticulous would *prefer* we not talk about."

"You mean on top of everything else, Meticulous controls what Mes talk about too?" I asked.

"That's why we meet in secret," said Steampunk, grabbing a few Headachies from Motor's bag. "Plus, we don't get invited to many Me parties."

"So what aren't we supposed to talk about?"

"For starters, why there's the Void outside the hotel," said Alien Abduction.

"Are you for real? You think the darkness outside is a void? As in, nothingness? You've peeked your head out the door and seen it firsthand?"

They looked at me like I'd just suggested we all slather our shoes in salsa and eat them whole.

"That would be suicide!" said Monk.

"And besides, the doors have alarms," said Steampunk. "Even if the Void didn't kill us, we'd get busted for sure!"

Motor blushed. "Look, I doubt there's a void out there. But I'm not willing to test the theory."

"Don't be a sucker!" said Alien Abduction. "We have proof of the Void! The Missing Mes!"

"Who?" I asked.

Steampunk's goggles filled with tears. "Mes who Meticulous got rid of. Some of them were our friends. Like Disco Me."

"Yeah, and he was a real genius," said Motor. "I mean, despite the disco. But that wasn't his fault. Culturally, his Earth is stuck in the 1970s. Anyway, he helped his version of Mom and Dad invent all kinds of stuff, like a cold-fusion generator and a holographic projector. Way cool."

"Sensitive Me wasn't any slouch either," said Monk. "He created the first self-driving car on his Earth. And the interactive public toilet."

I might have been more impressed if I hadn't seen those inventions already on Earth One. "And now they're just . . . gone?"

"Without a trace," said Alien Abduction. "I heard that Meticulous sent them through the Exit himself."

"That's just a rumor stemming from lots of bad vibes and negative energy," said Monk. "No Me could actually do

that to another. Meticulous can't be *that* bad."

Steampunk adjusted his floppy bow tie. "Maybe, but it's easy to see why he'd want Resist Me out of the picture. All that talk of change and rebellion."

Motor cut his eyes at me. "The fact is, nobody can figure out what happened to the Missing Mes because we're not allowed to talk about it."

"I just don't get why you all would—"

"Why we'd put up with Meticulous and his stupid rules?" Motor finished.

I grinned. "You took the words right out of my mouth."

Before I got an answer, the door burst open and in rushed Troll Me, the jerk who'd given Motor a hard time. "I've found Wild Me!" he shouted into his MeMinder. "He's in the ice room. Hurry!"

Monk nearly tipped over in his chair. "You're Wild Me!"

Alien Abduction sat up in his seat. "The one Meticulous is after?"

Steampunk scooted away from me. "So, wait, is that, like, angry-wild or out-of-control-wild?"

"I'm just me, okay?" I jumped to my feet.

Troll braced himself against the doorframe, blocking my way out. He cackled like a scrawny supervillain. "And now, thanks to me, you're caught! Motor, you're about as good at hiding troublemakers as you are with computers. That is to say, you suck!"

My hands started fizzing again, and I knew what to do. In one fluid motion I picked up the plastic garbage bin near the door and slammed it over Troll's head and shoulders. It was the kind of nimble move that should have been beyond me, but I felt I could do anything. Maybe all Mes felt this, and maybe that's why everybody else had accomplished

110

more than me. I got so distracted by this idea that I almost didn't take the time to enjoy the sight of Troll bonking into the wall as he tried to get out from under the bin.

Laughing like a reverberating guitar, the Why Mes and I ran out the door that Motor held open for us. We left Troll behind to spin around the room. The other Mes rushed off one way down the hall, and I went the other. I figured they wanted nothing to do with Wild Me, Average Me, or whatever kind of Me I was.

After a few steps, I heard Motor's cart whirring from behind. He almost crashed into me when I stopped to face him. "Why are you following me?" I said. "Go save yourself!"

Motor zipped his cart up to a beat-up old metal door that creaked when he opened it. On the other side lay a grubby cement stairway leading into the cold darkness below.

"You need the elevator, right?" he said. "I know a shortcut."

★ 19 ★

Mole Mes

The utility tunnels underneath the Janus were a hot and stinky maze of grubby cement and flickering lights. Pipes and gauges stuck out everywhere, and the ceiling hung back-achingly low. The snaking passageways twisted and turned and looped on each other in ways that made no sense. But deep down in this nasty dungeon, I felt safer than I'd felt all day.

"Not even Meticulous knows about this space," said Motor, squeezing his cart through a spot where two thick air ducts bulged toward each other. His ride wasn't exactly made for traveling in such close quarters. It had been hard enough helping him lug the thing down the stairs.

Every time we passed under a venting grate, I caught

snatches of dumb conversations from Me Con panels like "Crappiest Christmas: Most Disappointing Gifts," "Barf on the Beach: Which Family Vacation Was the Worst?" or "Epic Farts: Our Best of the Best." They all sounded like such wastes of time. Mes could have explored so many more meaningful topics if they'd just stop bowing down to Meticulous. Together, they could crack the mystery of the elevator, uncover the secret of the Void, figure out Algebra II. There was no end to the possibilities.

That said, I had to admit I was a little curious about the fart panel.

But for now, the only question that mattered was how much closer this tunnel would take me to the elevator before it petered out.

"Thanks," Motor said after I helped him navigate an especially tight section. "And thanks for taking care of Troll back there. And at that panel too. I never realized Diarrhea Delights could double as slingshot ammo."

"What is it with him? Why's he so mean to you?"

Motor broke into a tube of Chemically Flavored Crunchies. "He's had it in for me ever since I corrected his coding for a computer virus he was showing us at a panel last year."

"A virus? That sounds dangerous."

"It was just a minor thing that lets you take over the school's computer. Straight As and perfect attendance with a few keystrokes."

"That's minor?"

"Child's play for him. His idea of fun is hacking game servers and stealing virtual money from players with codenames he doesn't like."

"He's a real stand-up guy, in other words."

"The worst." Motor polished off the last of the Crunchies. "So why does Meticulous have it in for *you*?"

"Beats me. I mean, sure, I went to his Earth, but I left it just like I found it, more or less."

Motor screeched to a halt. "You went to another Earth?! To *his* Earth?!"

"It was the first place the elevator took me."

Still in shock, Motor started inching forward again. "How did it take you there, exactly?"

"I just pressed a random button. I was in a rush. Didn't know it was against the rules."

Motor was so stunned he shoved a trayful of leftover gum wads in his mouth instead of the Sodium Headachies he'd been going for. He spat them out, then got right back to the chips. "All this time only Meticulous has been able to take the elevator to other Earths. The controls don't respond to anybody else. Trust me, we've all tried. It only takes us straight to zero, then back to our Earths."

"What if a Me tagged along with another Me on his ride home? I think that's what Hollywood did with Meticulous so he could work as his assistant."

He tipped the crumbs at the bottom of the Headachies bag into his mouth. "Sure, it's possible, but generally, Meticulous always posts Mobster or some other guard at the elevator to make sure we only ride one at a time. He says more than one Me on any given Earth is too 'messy.' What a hypocrite!"

"So how is it that I can control the elevator like Meticulous? I'm nobody."

Motor finger-scraped junk-food sludge off his teeth. "Well, you're from the last Earth the elevator can reach. Maybe that makes you special somehow. How long were you on his world, anyway?"

"Long enough to realize I had to get out of there. It was creepy. He practically runs the whole planet."

The tunnel ended the way it began: in another grubby cement staircase. Motor had to get out of his cart again so we could heave the contraption up the steps. We were both wheezing by the time we got to the top. Motor plopped himself back into his seat as I cracked open the door and peeked outside. We'd come to an intersection of boring brown hallways, each one exactly alike in every direction.

I stepped back to let Motor inch through the door. Once out, he pointed left. "That way leads to the Viral Me Lounge. Nobody's scheduled to be there now. If you slip inside, there's a door at the other end of the room that leads right to the elevator bank."

We both froze as something metallic clinked around the corner. I hadn't passed through the door yet, and Motor had the good sense to kick it most of the way shut just before Ren Faire jogged up to the spot where I would have stood. I peeked in on them through the crack.

"Prithee, fat one." Ren Faire gripped the hilt of his sword like he might pull it out. "Hast thou seen the scoundrel known as Wild Me?"

Motor took a moment to lick the candy dust from an empty Cavity Pellets bag. "Nay, alas and alack."

Ren Faire dropped his Elizabethan voice. "Hey, only I get to do Shakespeare around here! Got it?"

"Nay, I speak not in jest, good sir! This is how people doth converse on mine Earth."

Ren Faire scowled. "Hast thou anything to do with a certain illegal discussion group known as the Why Mes? They were caught harboring the knave."

"Nay." Motor wadded up the bag and tossed it at the nearest trash bin. He missed. I would have too from that distance.

Ren Faire took in Motor's belly, and his face scrunched in disgust. "Thou shouldst be ashamed to call thineself a Me." And with that, he jogged away.

As soon as the coast was clear, I stepped out. Motor hunched in his seat, wiping the wet from his eyes.

"Don't listen to him," I said. "He's a jerk. Let's go."

Motor shook his head. "Those halls are even tighter in some places than the tunnel was. My ride won't fit."

"Then ditch it."

He patted the steering wheel. "I'm spoiled by it, I guess. Anyway, we both know I'm a lost cause. I'd just slow you down."

"Don't say that. You're awesome, and Ren Faire's an idiot. I couldn't have gotten this far without you."

"Nah, I'd just slow you down." All of a sudden, his face brightened with an idea. "But I can give you a decent distraction."

He aimed his cart in the direction Ren Faire had just run.

"Don't! It's too dangerous!"

But he zoomed off without so much as a backward glance.

I understood. I was bad with goodbyes too.

★ 20 ★

Feast Your Eyes on Me

When the sight of ninety-something copies of yourself eating dinner in a banquet room doesn't even make you blink, you know you've been traveling the multiverse a little too long.

Peeking in on the Viral Me Lounge through the service door, I wasn't scared, stunned, amazed, giddy, or any other emotion a sane person should have felt at seeing something like this. I was just annoyed. These Mes weren't supposed to be here. They sat under a banner that read ME APPRECIATION FEAST, a dinner Motor hadn't known about when he'd sent me this way. Based on the chatter I overheard, Meticulous had organized it as a last-minute surprise party. Perfect timing.

All my counterparts gabbed away, as excited by a free meal as I would have been . . . if I hadn't needed to pass through this room undetected. The only Mes who seemed even less thrilled than I was with this turn of events were the Viral Mes. Dare Me and Click Me sat at the VIP table up on the stage, not bothering to hide the disgust on their faces. Troll Me sat with them, but he was too busy picking garbage out of his hair to join in the grousing. Apparently that bin I'd thrown on him had been especially messy inside.

Meanwhile, Hollywood plodded from table to table, delivering food and taking orders for second helpings. He looked miserable. I'd almost forgotten how Meticulous had punished him into being a waiter, but I didn't have much sympathy. It was a slap on the wrist compared to what Meticulous had in store for me. I wasn't keen on being sent through the Exit and becoming a Missing Me. I just wanted to get home, preferably before Mom and Dad noticed I'd been gone. Now, with my shortcut to the elevator ruined, I'd have to backtrack.

Hollywood passed close by the door, pushing a cart stacked with platters of pizza. Most of them looked like standard cheese-and-pepperoni affairs, but I saw a few toppings that only somebody from another dimension could love: Frosted Flakes pizza, rainbow Jell-O pizza, potato salad pizza, and other horrors.

Seized by my dumbest idea yet, I leaned into the room just enough to wave Hollywood over while nobody else was

119

looking. He nearly dropped a mayonnaise-and-banana pizza at the sight of me. After staring way too long, he finally wheeled his cart over to the door and slipped through.

Up close, Hollywood didn't look so hot. His face had ballooned like instant biscuit dough in an oven. He might have been glaring at me, but it was hard to read any expression on his inside-out-watermelon face.

"What happened to you?" I asked.

Hollywood made what I assumed was an embarrassed look under all the lumps. "It's your bag of Diarrhea Delights. I'm allergic."

Served him right, but I felt kind of bad for him just the same. It's hard to stay mad at a moronic Xerox of yourself. "So, how's the job treating you?"

Hollywood stuck out his lower lip, which had grown to the size and shape of a peeled tomato. "It's fine, thanks." He couldn't sell this lie for anything—some actor.

"But it has to stink to be a waiter in the club you started."

"Fudge! This is only temporary! Meticulous and I just had a misunderstanding. Once he comes back to Me Con, which should be any minute, I'll explain myself and get back my job as his assistant. Then I'll be at the VIP table again in no time."

"Yeah, to serve them dessert. Face it: you're not a Viral Me anymore. You're at the bottom of the ladder now.

There's no future for you at Me Con." I probably should have eased into this, but there wasn't any time to soft-pedal.

Awareness seemed to penetrate the bloated shell of Hollywood's head. Tears welled up in his eyes, and his overgrown lips trembled. Bingo. Time to go all in. "Thing is, I know a way we can stick it to Meticulous."

Hollywood's swollen ears perked up as he listened to what I had to say next.

★ 21 ★

Feed Me

I swore to myself that if I ate half as disgustingly as the Mes stuffing their faces in the Viral Me Lounge, I'd watch a tutorial on table manners as soon as I got home. All the lip smacking and flying food bits skeeved me out so much I could hardly look at any Me long enough to get their orders. Not that I was taking their orders for real. I was only a fake waiter, after all.

Hollywood and I had found a nearby linen closet with a spare waiter uniform that I slipped on over my clothes. That let me move through the lounge alongside him without raising suspicion. No one recognized me, but I had to stack the dirty dishes and pizza trays on the cart and listen to complaints about bad service. Still, I'd have preferred that to hearing Hollywood crack his knuckles.

"This gosh-darned plan will never work," he muttered, popping both thumbs at once.

"Can you not do that?" I asked.

"What, swearing? Look, I know I have a potty mouth, but I'm under a lot of stress!"

"No, I mean cracking your knuckles. I kicked the habit last year, and I don't want to start again."

Glaring straight at me, Hollywood cracked every finger on both hands, one at a time.

The two of us bickered our way through the ballroom until we reached the VIP table. Just behind it was the exit door. All we had to do now was sneak past Click, Dare, and Troll, plus whoever might be guarding the elevator.

As soon as Troll saw us approach, he slapped his peanut-butter-and-squid pizza back on his plate. "Great, thanks so much, Hollywood! Your messed-up face just ruined my appetite!"

"Not mine!" said Click. "Bring me another pork soda, Mush Face!"

Hollywood threw an empty pizza tray to the floor with a clatter. "You guys were nothing before I took you under my wing!"

Having a hissy fit wasn't the coolest move. The Viral Mes laughed and the nearby tables joined in. Hollywood looked set to tell them all off, until I pointed to the door, our ticket to the elevator. "It's now or never," I whispered.

Hollywood took a deep breath to calm himself, then nodded. We were just about to make a break for it, when the main doors burst open with a bang and Ren Faire strode into the room. Head held high, he looked every inch the fancy-pants actor making his grand entrance.

"Duck!" I whispered.

I crouched behind the empty side of the Money Mes table without any of them noticing. But Hollywood just stood where he was, Gorilla Glued in place. He glared at Ren Faire as everybody else applauded and shouted out his name. Ren Faire raised his gloved hands for silence. "Thank thee, everyone. Sorry to be late, but duty doth call. Just a pit stop for me before I get back to mine pursuit of a dastardly villain."

Ren Faire strode up to Hollywood's cart and double-fisted two hefty slices of jelly-doughnut-and-chicken-feet pizza. Everyone laughed and applauded as he ripped a big bite from each slice and gulped them down, Henry VIII–style. At least he knew how to chew with his mouth closed.

"How now, Hollywood?" he said, dropping the half-eaten slices back onto the tray. "What happened to thine skin? Allergic to work?"

Everybody laughed again. Hollywood forced a smile, but he couldn't mask the hate on his inflated face.

There was no way Hollywood could leave here unnoticed now, but I still had a chance. I could slip away while all the Mes watched Ren Faire make a fool of him. Sure, I'd promised Hollywood a way out, but what could I do for him if he wasn't willing to follow the plan?

I was getting ready to make a run for the door when

Ren Faire wrapped an arm around Hollywood and squeezed hard. The sight stopped me cold. It looked just like something Nash would do.

That settled it. I couldn't leave any version of myself in the hands of a bully.

As Ren Faire dragged Hollywood to the center of the room, I crawled under the nearby Toga Me table for a closer position.

"Prithee, Hollywood," said Ren Faire. "I understand thine little TV show hath been canceled. We are all so sad about that, are we not, everyone?"

The crowd made a collective "Aw!" sound before breaking into more laughter. Hollywood looked equal parts embarrassed and livid.

"Thou shouldst look on this as a new opportunity," said Ren Faire. "For instance, thou couldst try live theater. 'Tis much more challenging and fulfilling than TV."

Speechless either from nerves or the swelling in his hot-dog-size lips, Hollywood just nodded.

"Live theater happens to be mine specialty," Ren Faire continued. "Mayhaps we could do some for the crowd now. Prithee, doth thou know thine Shakespeare?"

"I guess," muttered Hollywood.

Ren Faire puffed out his cheeks like Hollywood's. "I guess!" More laughs.

I ducked under the Play Me table next, slithering around their toothpick legs until Ren Faire's boots were just within reach.

"All right, then!" said Ren Faire. "Let us do a scene from

Twelfth Night, shall we? Every real actor doth know that one backward and forward. Am I right, Hollywood?"

I couldn't see Hollywood's reaction, but judging by the new round of laughter from the crowd, it must have been pretty unconvincing.

"Excellent!" said Ren Faire. "We'll pick things up at act two, scene three."

Ren Faire cleared his throat.

Which was my cue to reach out from under the table and yank down his pants.

★ 22 ★

Chase Me

The entire lounge laughed at Ren Faire's dragon-print boxer briefs. The laughs turned to screams when I popped out from under the table. "Wild Me!" people shouted.

I grabbed Hollywood by the arm and pulled him toward the door. On the way, he kicked Ren Faire from behind so that he toppled over face-first in the middle of pulling up his tight leather pants.

We giggled as we darted past the Viral Mes, who were too stunned to stop us.

"After them!" cried Ren Faire, struggling to get up.

But we were already gone, flying through the door and flipping off the lights on our way out. Mes cried in the darkness as I slammed the door shut behind us.

I kind of figured they'd scream like that. I was afraid of the dark too.

Very few things at Me Con could have surprised me by that point, but one of them waited for us just outside the door. Motor circled his mobility cart around the unconscious body of Mobster Me.

"What's up?" Motor said with a little wave.

I prodded Mobster with my foot, much harder than I needed to. He didn't stir. "You did this!?"

Motor held up a bag of Diarrhea Delights. "He was heading to the elevator to guard it, so I shared some of these with him. After lacing them with melatonin."

I gave Motor a high five. "That's the sleep hormone, right?"

Motor nodded. "Restless Leg Me had plenty to share. He can't nod off without it."

"I'll be jitterbugged, if you'll pardon my dirty mouth!" said Hollywood. "The old tranquilizer routine. I thought that only worked in movies!"

Motor took in Hollywood's swollen face and whistled. "Amazing! I've never seen such a bad allergic reaction in a Me. Pomegranates?"

Before Hollywood could curse out Motor in that dorky way of his, the lounge exit flew open and Troll jumped through. My arms tingled again, giving me the strength to shove him back the way he'd come. I wound up pushing harder than I meant to and knocked him into Click and Dare. They fell in a tangle.

128

"Jeepers!" said Hollywood, so stunned he didn't even apologize for swearing. "You're not average in the strength department, I'll give you that!"

Motor looked more excited than surprised. "You should see his aim! He pegged Troll with a Diarrhea Delight from the far side of Ballroom C!"

"Forget about that. Let's go!" I raced for the elevator bank as Motor and Hollywood fell in behind me. We had a good head start, but Motor started to lag. His cart made clunking sounds.

The Viral Mes got back on their feet and rushed down the hall toward us. Behind them, a screaming-mad mob of Mes spilled out of the banquet room. Ren Faire hopped along in the middle of the crowd, still trying to pull up his pants as his sword scabbard slapped his bare legs.

Motor's cart slowed to a crawl. "Battery's shot!"

"You're almost there!" I yelled. "Just keep it floored!"

I reached the call button ahead of Hollywood and slapped it. The light blinked on, but the doors wouldn't open. We heard the elevator car rumbling toward us from above. "Jumpin' Jehoshaphat," said Hollywood. "It's in use?!"

Motor pulled up to us, his cart shuddering one last time before going dead. "The thing's toast!" He struggled out of the useless ride, tipping it over in the process.

The mob streamed down the hall toward us, dozens of faces sharing a rubber-stamped look of rage.

Hollywood listened at the elevator door. "I swear it's getting closer! Just a few more seconds!"

Motor slumped against the wall in defeat. "We don't have that kind of time!"

I don't know what possessed me to kick a four-hundred-pound mobility cart, but the fizzing in my legs made it seem like a normal enough thing to do. I just placed my foot on the hunk of metal and gave it a shove. The cart shot along the floor, flipped back on its wheels, and torpedoed toward the mob. Screaming, they scattered out of the way. Nobody got hit, but they stopped dead in their tracks just the same, afraid to come closer. Everyone stared at me like I was some sort of monster. "Wild Me!" they muttered.

Motor and Hollywood jinxed each other: "How did you—"

The ding of the elevator cut them short. We turned to the opening door, ready to jump inside. But somebody already stood there.

Meticulous.

He leaned against the control panel, smoothing his suit with a gloved hand. He didn't look at all surprised to see us. "What are you gits on about, then?"

"Let's go!" I shoved Motor and Hollywood toward the lobby.

"Onward!" Ren Faire yelled from somewhere in the Me mob. "Once more unto the breach!" The thud of nearly a hundred size 6 shoes started up again.

As soon as we hit the lobby, I made a

beeline for the employee entrance. Orange pylons and Do NOT CROSS tape blocked the door, but I shoved them out of the way and grabbed at the handle.

Hollywood stopped short. "Are you crazy?! That's the Exit! The Void's on the other side!"

"It's just a way out, and that's all it is!" I waved a hand toward Ren Faire and the rest as they ran straight at us, screaming bloody murder. "You prefer dealing with them?"

That was all the convincing Hollywood and Motor needed. They followed me as I plunged through the Exit.

★ 23 ★

Null and Void

The outside of the Janus Hotel might as well have been the end of the world. There wasn't a soul to be found. Not in the empty streets, the abandoned park, the deserted stores and restaurants. The place was a ghost town.

We three Mes had only a second to take in this strange scene before the door slammed shut. We all spun around in sync, like some kind of dancing boy band. The door handle had been replaced with a thick metal plate, but that didn't stop Hollywood from clawing at the thing to pry it open. It wouldn't budge. The boarded-up windows didn't look like they'd be opening anytime soon either.

The truth didn't just sink in—it body-slammed us: there was no getting back inside the Janus.

Hollywood's bumpy goldfish eyes popped in fear. "Fiddle-sticks! This is the Void?!"

"No." Motor pointed to the boards covering the Janus windows. "Meticulous just made it look like a void."

"The Void was a fake all along!?" said Hollywood. "Fudge!"

"I guess this place is just an Earth like any other," I said. "Except . . . empty."

Hollywood kicked the door so hard that he shook the SecureMe camera mounted above it. "Jiminy Cricket! Yeah, I said it! Who cares?! We're fudged!"

"Guess Meticulous didn't mean for anyone to get back in," I said.

Hollywood rubbed his foot, wincing in pain. "Where is everybody? What did them in? Radiation?! Poison?! Zika virus?! Zombies?! Are we next?!"

"If there was anything bad in the air, it would have seeped into the hotel through the ventilation," said Motor, breaking out a Bowel Blocker. "We would have known."

That's when I started fizzing again. This time it wasn't just in a few parts of my body, but all over. I even felt it in my eyes, ears, and nose. I could see the fine print on the nutrition label of the Bowel Blocker wrapper; smell the chemical mix of processed chocolate, nuts, and caramel; hear every munch inside Motor's mouth. Along with superstrength and superspeed, now I had supersenses. But I would have traded them all in for a blindfold when I looked up and saw what hung over us.

A crack spread across the sky, like a lightning bolt that got stuck before striking. It pulsed with dark green light that matched the rhythm of the fizzing. I couldn't explain why, but deep down, I knew this rip in the air had something to do with all the weird stuff going on inside me. If I stood directly under it too long, would I get radiation sickness? Would I turn green and sprout a third arm?

Hollywood nearly turned catatonic with fright when he saw it. "Wha-wha—"

"I think he's trying to ask what that is," said Motor. He seemed more fascinated than scared. "Any idea?"

"None. I think it's causing the fizz, though."

"Fizz?" asked Motor.

"You don't feel it?" I asked. "It's like that time at Aunt Julie's farm with the electric fence?"

"Oh yeah!" said Motor. "How can I *not* touch an electric fence, you know?"

"This isn't story time!" Hollywood waved at the crack. "We've gotta get away from that gosh-darned thing, if you'll pardon the language!"

"So you don't feel any effect from it?" I asked. "No fizzing?"

"I'm not *fizzing*," said Hollywood. "I'm just freaking out!"

Motor scratched some chocolate crust off the corner of his mouth. "Is this something you've felt before?"

"Since I got to Me Con. Before that, even. I guess ever

134

since Meticulous came to deliver the notes. It comes and goes, like adrenaline. But out here I feel it all the time. Am I gonna have a heart attack or something if this keeps up?"

"Oh gee willikers, he's mutating!" said Hollywood. "How do we get you to a hospital out here?!"

Funny thing about enhanced senses: you're so busy worrying about where your enhanced senses come from that you're too distracted to hear somebody sneaking up on you.

"Hands up and don't move!"

I knew the voice belonged to a Me, but I couldn't tell which one. It wasn't deep like Mobster's or dramatic like Ren Faire's or shrill like Troll's. That didn't make it any less scary. I raised my hands along with Motor and Hollywood, none of us daring to turn around.

"Who sent you?!" said the Me.

"Nobody," I said. "We left the hotel by ourselves."

"Why?"

"To see what the Void was all about?" said Hollywood.

The Me snorted. "You walked out of the Janus and into the so-called Void for a little stroll?"

"Wait a minute," said Motor. "Resist Me? Is that you?"

We all turned around to face a Me with long hair cut like a girl's. Not hippie hair. Not heavy metal hair. Girl hair, with bangs and lots of bounce. What's more, this Me wore a skirt. Not a kilt. Not a loincloth. A skirt.

This Me was a she.

135

★ 24 ★

Resist Me

My mind had already reeled a lot today, but Resist Me was a whole new level of reel. I knew a few transgender kids from school and it was no big deal, but seeing a transgender twin of myself hit a lot closer to home. Had I always just figured I was a boy but missed something? Was I in denial? And if so, did I have the guts to do something about it?

It was so much to take in that I barely registered the slingshot Resist aimed at us.

"Resist, old buddy!" Hollywood flinched every time his eyes landed on the slingshot. "How've you been?"

Resist pulled her weapon tighter, so we raised our hands higher. "Don't 'old buddy' me, you sellout! We were never friends, even before you started working for Meticulous! He sent you here, didn't he?"

"I got fired, okay?!" said Hollywood.

Even with her hands occupied, Resist managed to crack both her thumbs as if she knew it would annoy me. "A convenient story."

"This is Hollywood we're talking about," said Motor. "You really think he'd last long as Meticulous's assistant?"

"Hey!" said Hollywood.

Resist smirked. "You've got a point there. What I don't get is you, Motor. I always knew you were a wuss, but I never thought you'd stoop so low as to work for Meticulous too."

"First of all, we're not working for Meticulous," I said. "We're trying to get away from him. He wanted to banish me here."

"You mean to say you escaped by running to the place you were trying to escape from?" she said.

None of us had an answer for that one. Finally, Hollywood said, "Well, when you put it like that, it does sound pretty gosh-darned stupid."

Resist took me in with the same snide look Meticulous had mastered. "Are you that new Me I've heard about? The one they call Wild Me?"

I pointed to my name tag. "I'm more of an Average Me, really."

"How did you know about him?" said Motor. "You haven't been to Me Con for weeks."

"We monitor transmissions in the hotel. Picked up a lot of chatter about a Wild Me causing all sorts of chaos."

137

Motor's eyes went wide. "Did you say *we*?! Are the other Missing Mes here too?!"

"The Missing Mes are just a conspiracy theory," said Hollywood. "They're not missing. They were sent home because they weren't following the rules."

Resist aimed the slingshot at Hollywood's nose. An easy target, given the swelling. "That's what your friend Meticulous told you, is it?"

Hollywood squirmed. "Uh, yeah?"

She gestured around the barren street. "Does this look like anybody's home to you?"

"So what is this place, then?" I asked.

Somehow, Resist cracked all her knuckles without lowering the slingshot. "Welcome to Earth Zero."

Resist had the best withering glare of any Me I'd met so far, probably the best in the entire multiverse. It was the kind of look that didn't just shut you up; it scared you from ever wanting to talk again. "Time for you to shove off," she said, tightening her grip on the slingshot. "I can't risk the safety me and my crew have built for ourselves."

"The other Missing Mes really are here, aren't they?!" said Motor.

"Cool!" said Hollywood. "Are you guys like some kind of ragtag band of Mes surviving on your wits and cunning?"

Resist sighed and lowered her slingshot. "You're all too

stupid to be a threat. And my hand is cramping up. Just don't try anything funny. I'm a quick draw."

"Why did Meticulous kick you all out in the first place?" I asked.

Resist scowled at the memory. "I can't speak for the others, but in my case, it's pretty obvious. Meticulous likes a certain type of Me for Me Con, and I clearly don't fit that description."

"Actually, he said you were too mouthy and political," said Hollywood. "Hey, don't look at me that way! Those were his words!"

Resist shook her head. "I shouldn't even be having this conversation with you in the open like this. I'm outta here. You're on your own. The wall's not far. So go start a new life. Good luck." She turned to go.

"What wall?" I said. "There's stuff here? Other people?"

"Do they have sushi?" asked Hollywood. "I'm dying for a decent meal."

Resist jerked her thumb over her shoulder. "The wall's that way. It's your only option at this point. Trust me, that hotel ain't opening anytime soon."

Which is exactly when the door swung open and Ren Faire poked his head out. He took us all in with a dramatic double take. "Stand thine ground, knaves! Thou art henceforth mine prisoners!" Then, over his shoulder: "Compatriots, come hither!"

"He's got backup!" yelled Resist. "Run!"

She took off down the street. Hollywood and Motor

followed right behind her, though at a much slower pace. "Come on, Average!" Motor cried as he pressed forward.

I almost joined them, but I was tired of running. The fizz roared through me like a thousand energy drinks, and I knew I could take on Ren Faire. Even when Mobster and Troll stepped through the door, I had no doubt I could beat them too.

Troll looked up and down the empty street. Wherever the other Mes had gone, they'd made their getaway without a trace. "I guess this one will do for now, but I get dibs on Motor."

"We shall find yon fatso and the preening jester soon enough," said Ren Faire. "But Wild Me is special to the boss."

"Why are you even coming after us?" I said. "Didn't Meticulous want to send me here anyway?"

Ren Faire's leather gloves squeaked as he clenched and unclenched his fist. "That was before he investigated thine actions on his Earth. Now he hath more questions for thee."

I was too amped up from the fizz to say anything witty, so I settled for "You and what army?!"

The three Mes laughed. Their guard was down, making this the perfect time for me to leap into action. The trouble was that different parts of me leapt into different kinds of action, and none of them matched. My legs did a dropkick while my fists struck out with a punch and my face thrust forward in a head butt. Separately, all three would have been good moves, but together they worked against each other. I wound up all twisted and fell to the ground in a heap.

So much for superpowers.

★ **25** ★

Work Those Buns

My pathetic attempt at fighting gave the three evil Mes quite a laugh. Troll got so carried away he actually fell to his knees. So, in a way, I'd brought one of them down, at least.

Ren Faire sauntered over to me and pointed his sword at my neck. He stood so close I could have kicked his legs out from under him or punched him in the privates. But after such an epic fail, I had no confidence left. It was time to surrender.

Just as I started to get up, some instinct made me duck back down instead. A trail of smoke streaked through the space where my head had just been and hit Ren Faire full in the chest. The smoke bomb burst in a thick gray cloud,

142

sending the Me reeling. Mobster and Troll froze as the haze spread around them. All three of them coughed in harmony.

Through the fumes, I caught a glimpse of Resist ducking inside a defunct business called Planet Fitness Cinnabon. She must have had a change of heart and wanted me to follow her. With my legs still supercharged, I rushed into the place. I'd eaten at Cinnabon and seen Planet Fitness, but I'd  never imagined the two going together. The thick stench of ancient sweat and stale frosting nearly knocked me out. By the door was a glass case of rotting pastries, and just beyond it, an abandoned workout room with busted exercise equipment. The ruined treadmills and StairMasters had little toasting pads attached to keep cinnamon buns warm as patrons worked out.

A clang and a muffled curse came from the doorway at the far end of the room. Resist must have stubbed her foot as she made her way through. "Wait up!" I called.

"Stay away!" she hissed.

So, of course, I didn't. No sooner had I leapt into the weight room than she came at me. I ducked out of the way with a pretty good dodge for somebody who'd barely ever been in a fight. But I was still too new at this to protect myself when she pinned me against a rack of dumbbells shaped like cinnamon buns.

"Thanks a lot!" She dug her forearm into my throat. "Mobster and the rest would never come this deep into the Rip Zone if Meticulous didn't really want you. Why is that?"

"Long story," I wheezed through my blocked windpipe.

She sneered. "If they find our HQ because of you, you'll really, really regret it. And I mean *really* regret it."

I gagged a little extra so she'd let go. It worked. "This is your HQ?" I spluttered, catching my breath. "Doesn't the smell get to you?"

She eyed the exit door. "This is just a hiding place. You'll never see our actual HQ, because you're leaving. I get a ten-second head start."

The front door banged open, and heavy footsteps stomped into the room we'd just left. "Youse can't hide from us, Wild Me!" yelled Mobster. "And neither can youse, pretty princess! May as well call it quits, or I'll plug ya!" Then a loud thunk, followed by an echo of the curse words Resist had used just a moment ago.

I peeked through a crack in the wall to see Mobster pulling his foot from the spokes of a fallen exercise bike. Resist shoved me out of the way and looked for herself. She whipped the slingshot from her pocket like she planned to shoot him through the hole. But before she could so much as load the thing, I snatched it out of her hand with my boosted reflexes. The problem was I forgot about my boosted strength—my fizzing grip accidentally snapped the weapon in two.

Resist slapped the broken weapon from my hand. "What kind of weirdo are you? Now I have to use my fists!"

"Are you serious? He's like twice our size!"

She rolled up her sleeves. "Nobody calls me pretty princess and gets away with it!"

"Let me try something else first."

I fished a quarter from my pocket and tossed it through the hole. Normally, I had the hand-eye coordination of a sea slug, but that wasn't the case in the so-called Rip Zone. For once in my life, an object I threw landed exactly where I wanted it to: right beside Mobster. As he swung his thick head around to see what had thunked beside him, I made a screeching noise. Mobster screamed and almost impaled himself on a rowing machine in his rush to get through the front door.

Resist screwed up her face. "What was that sound you made?"

"My rat impersonation. Rats scare me, so I figured they'd scare him too."

She grunted at me, with either grudging respect or deep annoyance. Maybe a little of both.

"Where to now?" I asked.

Resist brushed grit and plaster off her skirt. "You're not following me."

"Come on! I need to find Motor and Hollywood before the goon squad does. We're lost out here without you."

She stretched her legs to prep for running. "Not my problem."

I tried stretching too, until I pulled something in my

back and gave up. "Can't you see we're on the same side? We've both been kicked out of Me Con. Meticulous is our enemy. It only makes sense for us to team up."

Resist shoulder-checked me as she headed for the exit door at the far end of the room. "Meticulous wants you for questioning, and when he wants a Me for questioning, he won't stop until he gets his answers. I can't have you leading him to my crew.

"Sorry, Average Me," she said on her way to the back door. "You're on your own."

★ 26 ★

Earth Zero

Resist hadn't even touched the sticky door handle of the Planet Fitness Cinnabon exit before we heard footsteps fill the lobby. A quick glance through the hole in the wall showed Ren Faire and Troll searching the place for us. Mobster cowered at the entrance.

"Careful!" said Mobster. "Those rats could be anywhere! Real rats, I mean, not dem dirty rats we're after!"

Ren Faire spotted me through the hole and raised his sword. "Onward!"

I caught up to Resist so fast I crashed into her. We busted through the back door together as a mishmash of compatible body parts.

The back of the building butted up against a high

cement wall with rings of barbed wire on top. We couldn't go around, and we couldn't go back, so we had to go over. That looked impossible, until I saw Resist do it. With epic parkour skills, she bounced her body back and forth like a Ping-Pong ball between the wall and the back of the building, making her way up and then over the whole shebang.

I'd never done parkour, but now I had every reason to try. By the sound of the goons' stomping and shouting, they had nearly reached the exit door.

Jump, kick, jump, kick. It was official: being on Earth Zero had turned me into something far more than average. Before I knew it, I'd cleared the top of the wall. But seeing what was on the other side made me want to jump right back over.

I landed in a too-much-Halloween-candy nightmare interpretation of my town's Main Street. New buildings had sprouted up alongside the old ones. Next to the drab library rose a

castle. It wasn't just some prop but the real deal. So was the full-size pyramid beside the boxy courthouse, and the classic Japanese pagoda across from the ugly Department of Motor Vehicles. They were honest-to-goodness architectural marvels crammed up against squat little strip malls and gas stations. Even weirder, people were running businesses out of them. Smokey's Indoor Tanning & Barbecue had set up shop in a genuine Greek temple, while Chattering Teeth Dentistry & Trampoline Park took up the lower level of a French palace.

The stores themselves made even less sense. A place called Accordion Emporium sold nothing but five stories of wall-to-wall accordions. Dream Memes hawked what it claimed were custom dreams that played in your mind as you slept. A beauty salon offered treatments to make your hair burn like an eternal flame, and an auto garage touted itself as the "Best Hovercar Repair & Flying Frozen Yogurt in Town!" Even the familiar places were a little off. Bed Bath & Beyond had turned into Bed Bath & Bass Pro Shop, selling home decor and fishing supplies. Chick-fil-A had become Chick-fil-A Cheesecake Company, where fried chicken was stuffed inside rich desserts. And in place of the old Panda Express was a Panda Estée Lauder, where you could buy Chinese takeout and makeup.

As I stood there gawping, I got a faceful of feathers from a pair of giant wings passing by. They grew from the shoulders of some guy in a business suit. It turned out that a winged businessman hardly stood out on this sidewalk. An entire family with green skin and forehead antennae walked past us, followed by a little old lady with a glowing red eye implant and a robot arm. Across the street, a teenage boy and girl with the heads of Chihuahuas did skateboard tricks on the curb, nearly bumping into a real-life centaur cantering past them as he sipped from a bottle of homemade kombucha.

Even the normal humans looked bizarre, dressed in all sorts of insane clothes, from animal furs to astronaut suits. Some of their outfits didn't match at all, like a guy who wore a polyester leisure suit over Spanish conquistador armor, or a woman clad in a baby-blue tuxedo and an antique diving helmet.

"What is all this?" I asked Resist. She was busy listening for any sound of Ren Faire and the others trying to make it over the wall. I couldn't hear anything, thanks to the floral-print zeppelin that buzzed overhead. It was piloted by a guy in brass goggles and aviator leathers— a sight that would have driven Steampunk Me bonkers with excitement.

"Coast is clear," she muttered. "They're not following us." She motioned for me to join her as she started walking. "To answer your question, Earth Zero is the place where lots of Earths—too many Earths—combine into one. People, buildings, animals, technology, and things you can't even imagine got ripped from their original Earths and dumped here, forced to live side by side."

Half a block away, a robot barista outside a McStar-bucks argued with a black-robed witch about the amount of cauldron smoke spewing from her medieval hut next door.

"But how is all this possible?" I asked.

Resist fished an oversize coin from her pocket and tossed it to a team of break-dancing bishops we passed. "That crack in the sky over the hotel? They call it the Rip. Scientists here think it's a tear in the fabric between worlds."

"How did it open up?"

At the corner up ahead, a kid with a tiny dragon on a leash dumped a bottle of water over his pet's big flaming pile of poop before scooping it into a bag.

"Nobody here knows. But it happened three years ago. Does that timetable sound familiar?"

"That's when Me Con started!"

"The same time Meticulous creates an elevator that can travel between dimensions, dozens of dimensions just happen to converge on this world. And not just the boring Earths the elevator can reach, but really wild ones. Places almost unfamiliar to us."

On the street, a pumpkin carriage straight out of "Cinderella" crashed into a giant nuclear submarine on wheels. Traffic ground to a halt. Cars, hoverbikes, kids in pogo-stick boots, and floating-manta-ray riders started honking and shouting.

Resist had to raise her voice over the crowd. "Too

much of a ruckus. I like to keep a low profile. We'd better leave."

"As in, leave together?" I tried not to sound too hopeful.

Resist grunted in the snottiest way imaginable. "I can't shake you, so I guess I'm stuck with you."

★ 27 ★

Fight Me

Resist hurried me past a delivery person adjusting the straps of her jetpack and a parent group pushing strollers with furry yeti babies inside. Compared to them and everything else we saw on the way (roller-skating samurais, a "dirt spa" for plant people, a Toe Clippings "R" Us store), we didn't stand out in the slightest.

A few blocks later, we came to a boarded-up Star Trek Wars Cantina and slipped inside. The place combined *Star Wars* and *Star Trek* in bizarre ways. Statues of Darth Spock and Captain Kirk Skywalker greeted us at the door. Posters of Wookiees in Klingon battle gear and Vulcans in Stormtrooper armor lined the walls. The tables were shaped like spaceships that merged parts from the

Millennium Falcon and the *Enterprise*. Tattered old menus featured items like Beam Me Up Yoda Soda and Kirk I'm Your Father Focaccia.

Up on the stage, under a banner reading MAY THE WARP BE WITH YOU, two Mes traded punches. One of them wore a teal terry cloth one-piece jumpsuit with a wide collar and gold chains. The other sported clown makeup and denim coveralls with oversize leather boots and a Stetson hat. Motor and Hollywood watched from the sidelines. They sat next to a Me covered head to toe in a white lab suit, a filter mask, noise-canceling headphones, and thick plastic gloves.

Resist jumped up on the stage and broke up the fight, such as it was. Noticing her, Motor turned around and toasted me with a stale breadstick. "We were worried sick!"

Hollywood gave me the cold shoulder, barely glancing my way. "But not worried enough to go back out there and risk our necks."

"Speak for yourself," said Motor. "Once we stumbled in here, these guys wouldn't let us leave." He pointed to the Me in the jumpsuit. "That's Disco Me. And the other one is Rodeo Clown Me." He turned to the Me next to him. "And this is Sensitive Me. They're the Missing Mes!"

Sensitive sneezed into a tissue.

"Don't worry," Disco explained. "He's not contagious. He's just having a reaction to pomegranates."

Motor nudged Hollywood in the ribs. "We wouldn't know anything about that!"

Hollywood glared at him.

Resist cleared her throat for attention. "Disco and Rodeo Clown, that was an okay attempt at self-defense, but I need to see more progress at this point. And why were you just sitting there, Sensitive?!"

All you could hear through Sensitive's mask was some sort of muffled whining.

"No, that's where you're wrong," said Resist. "See, this *was* your fight. Every fight is your fight! You should have joined in!"

Rodeo Clown tightened the knot on one of his oversize shoes. "But that wouldn't have been fair. Especially since Sensitive Me gets overwhelmed when he has to touch people."

Resist glared at them. "You think Meticulous cares about fair?"

Nobody answered.

"We have to get our hands dirty if we're gonna have any chance of stopping Meticulous," she continued.

Hollywood scratched his puffy ear. "Stopping Meticulous? Are you crazy?!"

"This is for the good of all Mes!" said Resist. "For the good of all dimensions! Did you see what it's like out in Earth Zero?"

Hollywood pressed his fingers to his swollen temples. "Caught a glimpse. Still have a headache from it."

"The Rip, they call it?" said Motor. "How did it all happen?"

I told him what Resist had told me. Motor looked more and more upset the longer I went on. By the time I finished, Motor had gone as white as a Silly Me in mime makeup. "This can't be a Me's fault, can it?"

"It has to be some side effect of the elevator!" said Resist. "What else would it be?"

"Have you talked to the scientists here?" I asked.

Sensitive mumbled something, and Disco nodded in agreement. "We're trying to keep a low profile. If any of the locals ever figured out a Me was behind the Rip, there'd be hell to pay."

Motor looked sick. "What about deaths?! How many people has the Rip killed?"

Resist pounded a nearby table so hard a tray of C3-Picard cups tipped over. "No reported deaths, but so many lives have been uprooted! That's why we have to stop Meticulous! If we can get others to join us, we can free all Mes from his tyranny! Then we can force him to come back here and fix this place too!"

Hollywood whistled. "You sure are angry for a—" He caught himself before saying more.

The Missing Mes put their hands over their mouths in unison. Sensitive mumbled something that Disco translated: "Uh-oh!"

Resist gave Hollywood her most threatening look yet.

But rather than lay into him, she turned to the Missing Mes. "I need you three on guard duty. Those Viral Mes could end up finding our base this time. You know where to go."

Disco, Sensitive, and Rodeo Clown didn't look happy with their new orders, but none of them was willing to complain about it to Resist. Once they'd shuffled off, Resist turned back to Hollywood. "So I'm angry for a *what,* exactly?"

Hollywood's inflated face shook like a bobblehead. "Look, I've got nothing against guys wearing dresses or whatever. But since you're a Me, it's just confusing. I mean, does this mean I'm really a girl too and I just don't know it yet?"

"Since you're an idiot, am I an idiot?" said Resist. "Since Motor's a wuss, am I a wuss?"

Motor turned the familiar Me shade of red and stared at the floor.

"Hey now!" I said. In truth, though, I'd wondered the same thing about my own potential for wussiness since meeting Motor.

"Can it, Average!" said Resist. "You're the most confusing one of us all! How did you keep up with me when we escaped together? And how did you get over the wall? Only I can do that move!"

"What are you, jealous he's more athletic?" Motor said.

"I'm just concerned he's taking steroids or something," said Resist. "Not even the Fit Mes could have pulled off what you just did out there."

"Well, I had a little help." The words I needed were slow to arrive. "You see—"

"He has superpowers," Motor finished for me. He described how I'd kicked his mobility cart across the hall, and all the other things I'd done. Even I had to admit they sounded impressive listed together like that.

"Great Caesar's ghost!" said Hollywood. "I only now realized: Average is All of Me! Just like the legend says!"

Resist made a fart noise with her lips. "As if. You actually believe that nonsense?"

Hollywood shrugged. "Why not? We could use an All of Me right about now."

"I never went in for this All of Me business before," said Motor. "But if he does exist, I'd rather it be Average than anybody else."

Motor and Hollywood looked so hopeful I couldn't burst their bubble by telling them they were completely wack. No way was I some sort of legendary Me. Still, it was nice to be thought of as special for once in my life.

"But you're supposed to just be . . . average!" said Resist.

Hollywood laughed. "Yep, she's totally jealous!"

Something snapped in Resist. "I'll show you something

to be jealous about!" She took a step toward Hollywood, pounding her fist in her hand. He scurried backward, but he didn't get far. A Me who hadn't been there a second before now blocked his way.

Meticulous.

★ 28 ★

Screw Me Over

Meticulous didn't move a perfectly postured muscle as he stared us all down.

"Run!" Hollywood stumbled backward, nearly tripping over a life-size cardboard cutout of Jar Jar Borg.

"Relax," said Resist. She walked up to Meticulous and waved a hand at his head. Her fingers passed right through. "It's only a hologram." She nodded to a holo-projector propped up on a broken video game called *Phaser Saber Duel.*

Once she pointed it out, I couldn't miss the blank look on Meticulous's face and the stillness of his body. He was nothing but a projection of light.

"Sensitive hacked into the holo-communication relay

at the hotel a while back," said Resist. "This is the latest transmission to come through. He's projecting his image all over the hotel, and we're picking it up here too."

Recovered from his fear, Hollywood rushed up to the hologram, swung his butt around, and farted in Meticulous's face. Everybody laughed, except for Resist. "It's about to speak!" she said.

Holo-Meticulous came to life, the familiar self-satisfied look on his face again. "My fellow Mes, it's time for me and my assistants to leave you for a spell. You see, the elevator is a bit knackered, so I'm trying to build a new and improved one on a different Earth. The way the first elevator travels between our worlds is a little . . . *grotty*. All that going up and down between Earths has made a right botch job of the fabric between our dimensions. Only a few more trips in this old bucket and the portals to your Earths may collapse all at once."

"Sounds like Earth Zero times one hundred," muttered Resist.

"My new elevator will fix this problem. Once it's complete, we can travel the multiverse again without fear of mucking it up. We'll even be able to go beyond Earth Ninety-Nine. But the testing may take days, so you'll have to hang tight here. Travel back to your Earths is hereby suspended."

We four Mes gasped all together.

"He wouldn't!" said Motor.

"I overheard the Virals talking about some sort of plan," I said. "I never imagined this!"

Holo-Meticulous kept talking, oblivious to his audience. "That's right, mates. Vast new corners of the multiverse will open to us. Countless new Mes for us to welcome as brothers. But in order to reach these places, I need you to play a key role in this second phase of the Me journey by waiting here."

"I don't believe this!" said Hollywood.

"I do!" said Resist. "He doesn't care a lick about other Mes!"

Holo-Meticulous kept going. "You won't have to stay cooped up in this hotel, though. There's an entire world beyond the Janus. It's not 'the Void,' as your amusing rumors would have it. Rather, it's Earth Zero, and it's a brilliant place."

Hollywood ticked off a string of "gadzooks" and "fiddlesticks," and he didn't even apologize.

"In the meantime, my assistants have joined me for a final ride in the old elevator before I shut it down. But don't worry. I'll be back before you know it with a new and improved elevator, and a bold new era for all Mes! Ta for now!"

And with that, the hologram blinked out. Anger welled up in my throat so thick I couldn't swallow it down. "How could a Me do this to another Me?!"

Motor sank his forehead into his palms. "The longer I'm at Me Con, the less I understand about any of us."

"This whole idea of a new elevator sounds fishy to me," said Resist. "Hollywood, you worked as a little toady for Meticulous. Did he ever say anything about this?"

The swelling in Hollywood's face had gone down just enough to let him pout like I might have at age three. "I was his personal assistant, not his toady! And no, he didn't mention any plot. But I figured he had something cooking. He was always tapping away at this one MePad I was never allowed to touch."

That reminded me of the flash drive in my pocket. I pulled it out and tossed it to Resist. "I found this in Meticulous's office. It was shoved in a hidden holo-projector. Maybe there're notes or something worthwhile to see on it."

Hollywood looked even more hurt than before. "You mean you stole that right under my nose?!"

I patted him on the shoulder. "I'm sure you were a fine assistant, in your own way."

Resist turned the drive over in her hands. "Wait, you actually went to Meticulous's Earth?!"

"Long story."

Resist plugged the drive into the projector. It whirred for a minute, then shot out the hologram of a classic laboratory with test tubes, beakers, scales, and random machinery all over the place. A younger and somehow less serious Meticulous fussed over a big metal box with a dish-size hoop mounted on top like some kind of antenna.

Hollywood flicked a finger at Holo-Meticulous's nose, but it passed right through.

"This must be his holo-journal from a few years ago!" said Motor.

"That looks about right, judging by the haircut," said

163

Hollywood, fluffing his hair. "That's the slipshod work of Jason at Stylish Scissors Hair Salon. Remember him? Horrible fudging place, if you'll excuse my language. Can't believe Mom took us there. As soon as I got my hair done by a real stylist on the *Baker's Dozen* set, I never went back!"

Holo-Meticulous smiled at us. "This is experiment number twelve in my attempt to penetrate the barriers between dimensions! I'm most chuffed!"

"He almost sounds like a nice kid," said Motor.

Holo-Meticulous flipped a switch on the box, and arcs of electricity danced inside the hoop. Then the machine burst into smoke and flame. He swore up a storm and hurled equipment off the table.

"Maybe not such a nice kid after all," I said.

The projector jumped ahead in time to show other failed experiments that gave Holo-Meticulous just as many hissy fits.

"I could watch him fuss and fume all day," Hollywood said as Holo-Meticulous stomped yet another flawed edition of the hoop to bits. "But we might be here awhile."

"Controls!" Resist shouted. The projector beamed a holographic remote-control pad right at her fingertips. She tapped the Forward button, and the hologram skipped ahead, past an experiment that literally blew up in Holo-Meticulous's face.

"Rewind that!" said Hollywood. "This is worth it after all!"

"Let's try this instead." Resist sped the journal forward

to show Holo-Meticulous a little older and a lot more frazzled. The new hoop he'd built looked smaller and sleeker and stood on its own without the clunky box. "If this doesn't work," he said, eyes bulging, "I don't know what I'll do!"

"Pardon my French, but sheesh!" said Hollywood. "What a drama queen!"

Holo-Meticulous clenched his fists and tightened his jaw. "I can't fail! I swore I'd restore Mum's reputation. This has to work!"

"What's he going on about?" said Resist.

"His version of Mom died," I said.

Hollywood's puffy mouth drawbridged open. "He never told me that!"

Motor looked queasy again. "How did she die?"

"Wish I knew," I said. "Or maybe I don't wanna know. I'm not sure which."

Everybody nodded, too freaked out to say anything else.

Holo-Meticulous switched on the hoop, and an electric current crackled inside. "Yes! Yes!" The current turned green, the same shade as the light behind the elevator buttons—and, come to think of it, the Rip too.

Holo-Meticulous reached out to grab the strands of energy with his bare hands. At his touch, the beams of light bent and twisted like pipe cleaners. He leaned over the hoop to work with the stuff, blocking the view. Though I couldn't see what he was doing, the movement of his arms from behind looked familiar somehow.

"How's he doing that?" said Resist.

"And why hasn't the lightning fried him?" said Hollywood.

"It's not electricity," I said. "It's something else."

Holo-Meticulous straightened up, and I could see the hoop again. The energy he'd just fiddled with flashed in a burst of green light. When it dimmed, there was another world inside the hoop. A forest. It was like the view through a window. Meticulous shrieked with joy.

"Cool special effect!" said Hollywood.

Motor looked awed. "That's no effect. That's the first portal Meticulous ever made to another Earth!"

★ 29 ★

Holographic History

Holo-Meticulous was as giddy as a grade schooler showing off his Pokémon collection. We'd skipped ahead in his journal to a scene of him wiring his portal-making hoop into the Janus elevator. "If my calculations are right, the metal shell of this elevator should stabilize those energy fluctuations I encountered earlier! And now that the drive's plugged into the control panel, I won't have to adjust it by hand every time! I can just program a different destination for every button!"

"He lost me at *calculations*," said Hollywood. "Seriously, what does he mean?"

"Basically, this is where he got the idea to make the elevator a portal to other worlds," I said.

Holo-Meticulous pressed the Zero button. "I've viewed Earth Zero through the hoop, but this will be the first time I—or anyone in humankind—has set foot in another universe. From what I've seen, it's a lot like my Earth, so it's a good place to start."

We all tensed up.

"Earth Zero?" said Hollywood. "That's this world!"

As the elevator in the hologram started to move, a blast of green energy burst through the gaps and the car shook. "What was that?" said Holo-Meticulous.

When the elevator came to a stop, Holo-Meticulous jumped through the opening door in a panic. The holo-camera followed him as he ran through the hotel exit door, where a growing green rip tore the sky open. Then the holo blinked out.

For a while, no one said anything. It was a lot to take in. Here was proof that Meticulous, one of us, had rewritten an entire world. How many lives had he affected? How much damage had he done?

Finally, Motor spoke. He looked set to cry. "I'd almost come around to sympathizing with Meticulous after that stuff about losing Mom. Not now. He doesn't even want to clean up his own mess! He only sees the world he ruined as a convenient place to hold Me Con!"

"At least we can understand his mind-set a little better," I said. "He meant to 'restore Mum's reputation.' Instead, he caused a huge accident."

Motor shot me a vicious look, the kind I would have expected from Resist, not him. "What's the point of trying to understand Meticulous?! He's beyond help! End of story!"

"What gives?" Hollywood asked Motor. "I thought you were supposed to be the easygoing one."

Motor rifled through his bag for more candy but only came up with empty wrappers. He hurled them in the air, and they rained down on him. "Aren't you mad that a Me did this?"

"Well, I never bought into any of that 'we're all the same Me' nonsense," said Resist. "Look at the four of us. Beyond the same Mom and Dad, what do we really have in common?"

"Exactly," said Motor, brushing aside a Sodium Headachies wrapper that had stuck to his face. "What do I have in common with Hollywood? He's on TV. Resist, you're a natural-born leader. Average, you're All of Me, or close enough. And me? I'm just a fat kid in a mobility cart."

"Oh, come on!" I said. "You're smart. And you've gotten by without the cart just fine."

Motor slumped in his chair. "Barely. Trust me, as soon as we're out of danger, I'm going back to my crappy old habits—riding around and stuffing my face."

"If you're not happy with your *habits,* why don't you break them?" asked Resist.

Motor stared at the floor. "My shrink says it's how I've been coping . . . after the accident."

That shut everybody up. Motor didn't speak for a while, and when he finally did, the words came out as a whisper.

"Dad died. Something we were building went wrong. Way wrong. It got out of control, and . . . and . . . Dad didn't make it."

More awkward silence as the idea sank in. Dad dead after Motor screwed up. No wonder he had no faith in himself. No wonder the Rip got him so upset.

Finally, Resist spoke. "You all need to get over yourselves. I'm sorry about Dad, Motor. And I'm sorry about your candy allergy, Hollywood. And I don't even know where to begin with you, Average. I refuse to call you All of Me, by the way. The thing is, everybody's got something to deal with. And whatever it is, you've got to just accept it and move on."

"Well, since you bring it up," I said. "How about you?"

She rolled her eyes. "You think I'm torn up about the way I am? I'm not. And trust me, I don't have it easy back home. My Earth is way backward about this sort of thing. Mom and Dad are cool with it, in case you were wondering. But most people there aren't."

"That's all well and good," said Hollywood. "But do you have to act so crabby all the time?"

Resist leveled her scariest glare yet on Hollywood. But this time, he didn't look away. The staring contest went on until Hollywood started shaking, but by then he seemed to have passed some sort of test with Resist. When she spoke, she looked at all of us. "You know, you've really just got to figure this stuff out for yourselves. It's not my problem."

Then, for no apparent reason, she laughed. Then I laughed. Then Hollywood and Motor joined in. We all laughed as if in stereo, which made us laugh even harder.

In the middle of it all, two and two came together in my head, and I blurted it out: "The new elevator! He's building it on my world!"

"How do you figure that?" said Resist.

A big *Aha!* flashed across Motor's face. "If Meticulous wants to go deeper into the multiverse, he'll need to start at Earth Ninety-Nine, the farthest world the old elevator can reach!"

I thought about Mom, Dad, and Twig and swallowed my panic. "I've got to get back home! He could ruin it like he ruined this place!"

Motor's excitement drained away. "But Meticulous turned off the elevator after he left with the Virals. It's stuck on your Earth and can't come back!"

"I can bring the elevator back here," I said. "If it works for me the way it works for Meticulous, then I just need to press the call button."

"That's a big if," said Resist. "And we can't even get back inside the building. Door handle's been removed, remember?"

"Meticulous told everybody about Earth Zero," I said. "Maybe when somebody slips out, we can slip in."

It took a little more coaxing, but in the end I got Motor, Hollywood, and Resist to join me on a return trip to the Janus. Motor had demanded we take Sensitive, since he was "way smarter than me," but Resist nixed the idea. "He breaks out in hives when he goes outside." She ordered him and the other Missing Mes to stay behind and hold down the fort. They didn't gripe about it, at least not to her face.

Resist knew a shortcut back to the hotel, so Hollywood and Motor wouldn't have to jump the wall the way we had before. But once we crowded around the hotel exit, the door stayed shut.

"Why isn't anybody coming out?" I asked.

"They're wimps," said Resist. "Too many scary stories about the Void."

Motor slumped against the wall. "Then it's hopeless. We'll never get in."

An idea struck me. A dumb idea, but an idea just the same. I pointed to the SecureMe camera above the door. "That thing doubles as a projector, right? Anybody know how to turn it on?"

"The power button's way up there," said Motor. "Meticulous must use a remote."

I waved at the camera.

"Like I haven't tried that?" said Resist.

That's when the projector lit up, and another Holo-Meticulous appeared. He stood there as if waiting for us to say something.

Resist looked from the projection to the projector and then to me. "How'd you do that? I've been trying to get past this door for weeks."

"I don't know. Meticulous's desk responded to me too." Thinking about Mom's holographic memorial reminded me that it had to be past dinnertime back home. By now Mom and Dad would be filing a missing persons report. If I managed to survive this day, they'd surely kill me.

Hollywood gave Holo-Meticulous a wet willy. "Voice recognition enabled," said the projection. Hollywood shrieked and ducked behind Resist.

Motor slapped his forehead. "Of course! It's an interactive holo-lock! *Voice recognition* must mean it recognizes the voice of Meticulous or one of his goons!"

"Piece of cake. I tricked it once, I'll trick it again." I walked up to Holo-Meticulous. "Open Sesame!"

Holo-Meticulous smirked. "Voice not recognized. Disintegration ray enabled." A panel in the wall slid open, and the barrel of a gun popped out.

It aimed right at my chest.

★ 30 ★

Just Shoot Me

It felt so unreal to have a robotic ray gun pointing at me that I almost thought this had to be another hologram.

If only.

"Stand still!" Resist whispered.

I didn't move. Neither did anyone else, though Hollywood whimpered like a scared puppy.

"Why didn't it work?" I whispered, not taking my eyes off the gun. "I'm a Me, aren't I?"

"Same voice box, different accents and speech patterns," Motor whispered back.

"So somebody's got to trick the voice recognition," said Resist. "Average clearly isn't the one for the job."

"Hollywood, you've got to do it!" I said.

"Me?!"

"He's right!" said Resist. "You're always going on about how great an actor you are. Now's your chance to show us."

Hollywood started to cry. *"Baker's Dozen* only lasted one fudging season! *Pallin' with the Shaolin* was a straight-to-video flop! I haven't gotten any other parts since then, for Pete's sake!  That's because I stink at acting, just like Ren Faire says! Oh cheese and crackers!"

I didn't take my eyes off the gun barrel. "You're good at acting, and you should be grateful you have a thing. Me, I'm just . . . average."

"Give me a break!" said Hollywood. "You're All of Me! You've got superpowers and stuff!"

"Hardly. I can't control whatever's going on with me, or, believe me, I'd use it to escape."

The gun clicked like it was about to fire.

"Ten seconds remaining." Holo-Meticulous sounded almost giddy.

"Hollywood!" I said. "It's now or never!"

Hollywood shut his eyes and rolled his head around, making a bunch of weird faces and murmurs. It cracked me up when kids did these kinds of acting warm-ups backstage at theater class. Now it wasn't funny in the least. He was prepping for my impending death the same way he would for some scene from a sitcom! After what felt like forever, Hollywood finished and faced the hologram. He took a deep breath, blew it out in a very actorly way, then spoke. "Go ahead and bloody open up already, you toff!"

He crushed it. A first-rate impersonation of Meticulous, from the polished accent to the superior tone.

The dot on my chest disappeared, and the gun retracted into the wall as the lock clicked open. "Voice pattern recognized," said Holo-Meticulous, looking disappointed.

Everybody whooped except for Hollywood. He was so stunned, I had to prop up his hand for a high five.

"Next time you feel sorry for yourself, just remember how you saved me," I said.

Choking back tears, he nodded.

Resist moved toward the door, but Motor stepped in front of her. "Hold up! There were a lot of angry Mes after us before we came out here."

"We'll sneak around if we have to." I hoped I sounded confident. "Just so long as we get to the elevator. I know I can turn it back on."

"Good enough for me," said Resist, pushing Motor out of the way like he was made of packing peanuts. "Average, I'll give you cover. Motor and Hollywood, you get him to the elevator."

And before any of us could argue, she threw open the door and rushed in.

The entirety of Me Con had stuffed itself into the lobby of the Janus Hotel. More than ninety Mes. And all of them stinking mad.

From the door we watched the huge crowd shout out their gripes.

Cowboy Me: "What in tarnation kinda treatment is this?! That no-good, lousy snake in the grass done distracted us from goin' home! Me Appreciation Feast, my foot! Now we're stuck worse than a horse in a pool of molasses! Meticulous ain't never coming back for us!"

Military School Me: "He'll be back! He has to! He's our leader!"

Alien Abduction Me: "He's sold us out to aliens, man! They're coming in their mother ship to take us away!"

Monk Me: "Calm down! We've got to believe in the essential inner good of all Mes and trust that he'll do the right thing!"

They went on like this, every Me shouting over every other Me. Even the calmer Mes like Steampunk Me and Pool Hustler Me chimed in, though I couldn't make out what they said over loudmouths like the Fit Mes and Tune Mes. Through it all, a hologram of Meticulous stood frozen in the center of the room with that well-pleased face of his, like he was enjoying the chaos.

"We look so dumb when we argue," I whispered.

Resist ignored me as she scanned the room. "Anybody see Mobster in this mess? I'd just love to knock some sense into that oaf."

Hollywood slapped a fist into his palm, but he did it harder than he'd meant to and winced. "I don't see Ren

Faire either. Or Click and Dare. Got a gosh-darned bone to pick with them myself."

"Yeah, Troll's a no-show," said Motor. "Guess Meticulous took them along after all."

"As if!" said Hollywood. "They don't even know how he likes his coffee!"

I shivered at the thought of someone as violent as Mobster or as moronic as Click and Dare running loose on my world. What if Mom and Dad found one of them? No telling what damage Ren Faire or Troll or any of them would do to my life back home.

"I'm more than ready," I said. "Everybody else too?"

"There's no way!" said Motor. "We'd have to get past all those Mes!"

"Done," said Resist, stepping into the crowd.

"What are you doing?" Hollywood called after her.

Resist leapt at the nearest column, parkoured off it, flipped in the air, and landed on the check-in counter.

"Hey, Mes!" she said, standing up. "Word of advice: talking to yourself is a bad habit!"

★ 31 ★

Kick Me

Every identical eye in the Janus lobby locked on the check-in counter, where Resist took a long moment to smooth her skirt. After making them wait just a little too long, she spoke. "In case you don't know me, or conveniently forgot who I am, I'm Resist Me of Earth Fifty-Seven."

"You're a Missing Me!" shouted Kabuki Theater Me. "You were banished from Me Con! Why should we listen to you?!"

"Because Meticulous treated us Missing Mes like garbage, and he's not treating you any better. He's not coming back either, so you need a better plan than just standing around and arguing!"

Some Mes grumbled, some Mes nodded, but they all kept

their eyes on Resist. That was the idea—to give us the distraction we needed.

I stepped into the room and waved Motor and Hollywood to follow. "Come on!" I hissed. They wouldn't budge until I tugged them forward by the wrists. Once in motion, they kept behind me as I snuck along the back of the crowd. Resist held everybody spellbound, so no one noticed us.

"Meticulous lied through his teeth about why he brought us together for Me Con!" Resist shouted. "But he told the truth about one thing: together, we can be a force in the multiverse! Not a force for selfish greed, like Meticulous, but a force for good! Why should we settle for reminiscing in panels about our smelliest farts or overanalyzing our nightmares about otters when we have the power to change things? To change everything? The environment. Education. Income inequality. Racism and discrimination. By pooling the collective knowledge from our worlds, we can start to fix these problems and any others they throw at us!"

"How we gonna do that when we're stuck here?" said Restless Leg Me.

"Oh, we'll bust out of Earth Zero, all right!" said Resist. "And when we do, Meticulous will pay!"

Her words stirred up an equal mix of cheers and boos from the crowd. I didn't care how they reacted as long as we stayed under the radar. That turned out to be wishful thinking when Motor bumped into Monk by accident. I thought he might freak out at the sight of us, but instead he took us in and beamed. That was a relief . . . until he opened his mouth. "You're okay!" he yelled five times louder than he needed to. "We were so concerned, my brothers!"

What felt like all of Me Con looked our way. Why couldn't he have been one of those monks who take a vow of silence?

"Whoa there, hombre!" said Cowboy, clamping a hand on my shoulder. "You got yourself some questions to answer round these parts!"

Juvenile Hall appeared at my side. "Not cool, daddy-o!" He shoved Cowboy off me, then combed a few of his stray hairs back into place. "Don't even think about messing with Wild Me."

Cowboy shoved Juvenile Hall right back, pushing him so hard he fell to the floor. On the way down, Juvenile Hall bumped into Military School, who grabbed Monk's robes for balance. The two of them toppled into Alien Abduction, and everything dominoed from there. Soon enough, a fight broke out. It was like a gang rumble between infinite reflections in a dressing room mirror. Fit Mes versus Tune Mes.

Alterna Mes versus Play Mes. Work Mes versus Chill Mes. Toga Mes versus Look at Mes. And everybody piled on the Silly Mes, who fought back by throwing pies and shooting seltzer in their faces.

As distractions went, we couldn't have asked for better. We rushed to the elevator bank before anyone else saw us.

The call button had gone dark and stayed that way, even as Hollywood and Motor slammed it over and over. But at my touch it lit up like a refrigerator on a midnight snack run.

Hollywood fist-bumped me. "Gee willikers! The elevator really does respond to you. All of Me strikes again!"

Motor shushed him as he strained to listen at the elevator door. "Hear that? It's coming back from wherever Meticulous got off."

Hollywood shuddered. "Hope he's not on it this time."

We stood there waiting for an eternity, glancing back every few seconds at the Me war in the ballroom. If any Me saw us here, they'd demand to be taken home. We didn't have time for that, not if we wanted to stop Meticulous. Besides, if Meticulous was telling the truth, the old bucket didn't have many rides left before it went kaput. We'd be lucky to survive the single trip back to my Earth.

Finally, just when we were on the verge of three matching panic attacks, the elevator arrived in a shriek of metal on metal. The door only managed to open halfway, but at least the car was empty. I rushed in and went straight for the control panel, slipping my fingers around its metal frame. The screws weren't in tight, and it came right out with a tug.

"Can't you close the door?" said Hollywood, crouching in the corner. "I feel so exposed!"

"The controls are dead, and we're waiting on Resist,

182

remember?" said Motor, taking the panel off my hands. The wires connecting the buttons to all the gadgetry inside were too short to reach the floor, so he had to hold the big hunk of metal as I checked out the steel hoop it had covered. It looked dinged up and bent, but still workable.

Hollywood peered over my shoulder. "That thing isn't on, is it?!"

"Treat it like it is," wheezed Motor, straining from the weight of the panel. "We don't understand how it works."

"I think I do." Never mind that Meticulous was far more brilliant and capable than I could ever hope to be. At the end of the day, he was still a Me, which meant I should be able to figure out something he'd made.

Hollywood squinted at the device. "There's not even an On switch."

I ran a finger along the hoop, and green arcs of lightning sparked inside the rim. The strands of power merged together to form a glowing hunk of energy in the center, just like I'd seen in the holo. As my eyes adjusted to the brightness, I made out the shape of a giant padlock. I felt hypnotized by the sight of it. Almost in a daze, I reached for the lock.

A huge crash snapped me out of my trance, and I yanked my hand away. Motor had dropped the panel, ripping the wires loose and knocking out the buttons in the process.

"Motor?!" said Hollywood.

Motor's eyes bugged out. "The green lightning! It could've burned your hand!"

"No, it won't," said Resist, stepping into the elevator. She looked battered and bruised from her trip here through the fight, but any Mes who'd crossed her path were probably in worse shape. "Remember the holo-journal? Meticulous touched it and he was okay."

Motor looked over the broken panel and slapped his palm to his forehead. "I really messed this up! Sorry!"

No point in getting mad at myself. "No worries." I reached out again. When my fingers made contact with the energy, it felt like electric Play-Doh in my hands. I could stretch the stuff this way and that and mold it however I liked. But every time I let go, it snapped into the shape of a padlock again.

"So it's stuck like that?" asked Hollywood.

Resist peered down the hallway. "Just hurry up and figure it out!"

"I think it's a lock that needs a key," I said.

"Well, that's great," said Hollywood. "Where do we get a key?"

Just then a sheet of glowing green holo-paper appeared beside the padlock.

"It's right here!" I snatched the holo-paper from the air. "Or it will be." I started folding.

"You're doing origami?" said Resist.

I zipped through the first set of folds. "Yeah, it's an origami drive."

"The name of Meticulous's stupid band?" said Hollywood.

I shaped the key tip. "It makes sense when you think

184

about it. I found all those failed origami attempts in his office. And at my interview, he was really interested in my origami. Even recorded me making some."

"With a holo-recorder?" said Motor.

"Yep." I made a few final creases. "It wasn't much of a leap to realize that origami had something to do with the elevator. I mean, why else would he beat himself up trying to learn something he didn't even seem to like? At least, I'm assuming he doesn't like origami."

"Sakes alive, you guessed right!" said Hollywood. "It was the only thing he couldn't master. He hated that."

"Couldn't master?" asked Resist.

Hollywood winced at the memory. "He had a thing about being able to do all the stuff that other Mes could do. Karate, ceramics, kazoo playing, you name it. If a Me could do it, he had to do it better."

"That's our Meticulous," muttered Resist.

With a final fold, I made ta-da hands. I'd just folded a glowing green origami key.

"Seriously?" asked Hollywood.

I put the key in the lock, and they fused in a green blob. The light spun faster and faster. In moments the elevator hummed to life.

"It worked!" said Motor.

Military School chose that moment to stick his battered head through the door. "The Missing Mes! They're here!" he yelled over the shoulder of his ripped uniform. "And they got the elevator working again!"

Resist pushed Military School so hard he hit the far wall

185

of the elevator bank. When she looked down the hall, her eyes went wide. "We have to get this thing moving! A *lot* of Mes are headed this way!"

"And why shouldn't they?" said Military School, struggling to get up. "We have a right to use the elevator too!"

Resist raised a fist at Military School. That was enough encouragement for him to stay down.

"Average, do something!" yelled Hollywood.

As soon as I touched the spinning green energy, my entire being turned into a wave machine. Every atom in my body rippled. Just like when I stood under the Rip, I had the weird sensation of being connected to something bigger, only this time it was a lot bigger. It spoke to me, not in words, but ideas. And one idea in particular came up over and over: an octopus.

I folded the familiar shape in no time flat. As soon as I finished, the octopus spun in place, its green light almost blinding us.

"Motor, cover it back up!" yelled Resist. She grappled with three Fit Mes who'd rushed at the door. Hollywood jumped around behind her, waving his arms to distract them while keeping himself well out of punching range.

Motor banged what was left of the panel into place so we could see again. The elevator door had almost closed all the way when Cowboy slammed his gloved hand in the crack to make it rumble open again. Then a blur of leather and grease knocked him to the floor. Juvenile Hall pinned Cowboy to the ground, giving me a quick thumbs-up. "Go, go, daddy-o!"

"We'll come back for you!" I yelled as the door shut the rest of the way.

Rising up through the multiverse in a rickety box of metal, we four Mes should have been petrified. But we shared a different emotion, one that was written by the same pen all over our faces: guilt.

"That was cold," said Hollywood. "Leaving them all behind like that."

"Average, why'd you say we'd be back for them?" said Resist. "We can't promise anything like that."

Motor shook his head. "I feel like a turd."

I could have said lots of things at that moment. Lots of explanations, lots of excuses. But nothing would have sounded right. So I sighed and settled for the only other words that came to mind.

"Going up?"

★ 32 ★

Origami Overdrive

I always thought butterflies were the wrong bugs to stuff into a nervous stomach. For me, anxiety felt more like dung beetles crawling in my gut, rolling around their little stress balls of doubt, dread, and panic. A whole colony of them filled my digestive system as the broken elevator whined and screamed its way through ninety-nine dimensions. This was by far my worst ride through the multiverse yet, and it would probably be my last.

To distract himself, Hollywood checked his reflection in the metal of the control panel. The swelling had almost disappeared, though his face was still red and splotchy. "So, let me get this straight: to travel to another Earth, all you have to do is fold a crane or whatever, and boom, the origami drive takes you there?"

"Yeah, but there's more to it than that." I didn't know how to explain it, since *I folded the barrier between our reality and the next* isn't the kind of thing you just bring up in conversation.

"Basically, you're saying that each parallel dimension is represented by some animal shape?" said Resist. "Like an origami code? Doesn't that sound kinda silly?"

"Here's how I see it," said Motor. "It very likely takes some high-level math to calculate the position of each dimension. But if you plot out those numbers graphically— you know, serious geometry—they just happen to look like shapes we recognize. Our eyes fill in the blanks."

"Like seeing stuff in clouds?" said Hollywood.

"Yes!" said Motor. "The fact that they look like animals is just our minds finding patterns in the swirl."

"But the basic principle is you fold it one way, you end up in one universe," said Resist. "Fold it another way, you end up in another universe."

"Right," I said.

Hollywood rubbed his blotchy temple, like this gave him a headache. "So what's the origami code for my world?"

"A donkey?" said Resist. "A baboon?"

Motor and I laughed.

"Shut up!" Hollywood didn't actually sound too upset. He seemed to like any attention he could get.

"I don't know what to fold to get to your Earth," I said. "And I'm only assuming I made the right fold for my Earth. The octopus was an educated guess." I explained all the octopuses I'd seen in Meticulous's office, but left out how the multiverse had told me to fold one myself.

Resist whistled low, hitting the exact same note I always blew. "Meticulous had to calculate and then make the folds for a hundred worlds. Sounds pretty hard for a Me who doesn't even like origami."

"Must have been even harder to fold them the right way in the origami drive every time," said Hollywood.

"He just had to fold them once." Motor nodded at the busted control panel. "He had them preprogrammed in there, remember. But now all those folds are lost, thanks to me."

Resist shook her head. "Motor, stop moping already!"

But moping seemed like the only option any of us had left. Even if we reached Earth Ninety-Nine without breaking the elevator, I had no idea how we'd ever stop Meticulous and the other Mes he'd taken along.

The elevator screeched even louder as it started to slow. Everyone gripped the handrail, bracing themselves in a similar crouch, as if we'd picked the worst possible time to play monkey see, monkey do. Nothing like extreme terror to bring out the familiar in a quartet of interdimensional counterparts. When the car shrieked to a sudden stop, we nearly fell to the floor. The doors buckled open, and sparks shot from the origami drive. No sooner had we all rushed out into the elevator bank than something thick and clangy snapped up above. Everybody flattened against the far wall as the car broke loose from its cable and plunged down the shaft.

There, in the Janus Hotel of the Earth I called home, the four of us stared at the big empty hole where the elevator used to be. And as we looked, the fizz faded from my body and brain. I'd gotten so used to the feeling that I'd taken it for granted. Now it was gone, and with it, so were my powers. How could I fight Meticulous as just Average Me?

Motor tiptoed over to the busted doors and looked up and down the shaft. He whistled the way Resist had a few moments before. Hearing that familiar note from another Me destroyed any scrap of relief I might have enjoyed at making it home. I'd stranded him and the others here. All I felt now was a huge wad of shame.

"Before you tell us how bad you feel, save it." Resist looked down the hall to make sure we were alone. "Let's just focus on finding Meticulous."

"Where do we even start?" said Hollywood.

They all looked at me, expecting an answer.

"Not a clue," I said. "I mean, unless there's some other significant place for Meticulous to set up an elevator out there."

"What do you mean by *significant*?" said Resist.

I headed for the lobby and they followed. "He chose the Janus for his first elevator because that's where Mom and Dad met, right? The place has special meaning to him. To all of us."

The other Mes looked lost.

"You mean you never knew that?" I said.

"Wait, didn't Mom host her Physics of Traveling the Multiverse conferences here?" said Motor. "I knew she held them at some hotel, but I didn't realize it was the Janus."

"And I didn't know she was the organizer," I said. "I just figured it was some annual gathering of physics geeks."

We reached the lobby, the same space where—ninety-nine Earths away—we'd survived a massive Me brawl just minutes before. Now it was empty and creepy-quiet. The clock above the check-in counter showed it was just after dinnertime. I checked the time against the MeMinder. "Student Showcase in a half hour," nagged the device.

Motor made a beeline for a mostly empty vending machine in the corner. "Mom held two mini-conferences. She claimed she could prove travel between dimensions was possible. She did the experiments in front of all these other physics professors, but it didn't work either time. Kind of a major embarrassment for her, really. A career setback and all that. She was a laughingstock."

Hollywood looked hurt. "Why didn't she ever tell me that?"

Motor reached into his pocket and pulled out a disc of dirt with grass on one side, like a tiny clump of lawn. He tried to shove it into the bill acceptor. "This thing doesn't take green? Anybody else got some other kind of money?"

Resist scooped blobs of soft dough from her wallet, while Hollywood produced a slice of bread.

"Uh, sorry, everybody," I said. "But we use paper money

here. And coins. Mostly credit cards, I guess. And I don't have any of those things right now."

Hollywood took a bite of his bread money. "Hard to make change for pumpernickel anyway."

Motor shoved the dirt disc back into his pocket. "No problem." He pulled out a MePad, held it up to the machine, and started tapping buttons. "Anyway, Mom didn't tell me about her experiments either. I just read about them in her old notes and papers." He punched the Enter key on his screen, and all the junk food inside dumped into the dispenser tray. "It's not really stealing if this place is closed, right? Glad you all agree."

"So that means Meticulous didn't actually invent the elevator?" said Resist. "Mom did?"

Motor scooped out the loot. "Well, Mom laid the groundwork." He eyed his armful of snacks like a rich person might browse a wine cellar. "She did the math and wrote up the plans, but she couldn't pull it off and gave up. I'm guessing Meticulous fixed her mistakes."

"And took all the credit," said Resist.

With a Whatchamacallit clenched in his mouth like a cigar and a six-pack of Oreos under his arm, Motor tossed us the rest of the chips and candy.

I cracked open the side entrance door and took a peek. My bike was just where I'd left it. I'd known deep down that this was Earth Ninety-Nine, but it was good to get proof with my eyes.

I bit into a Kit Kat, good old familiar Earth Ninety-Nine

junk food. "Now it makes more sense than ever why Meticulous built the elevator at the Janus. He wanted to have a victory in the place where Mom had a defeat. You know, to memorialize her, or whatever."

Resist crunched a granola bar. "We get it—you have an uncanny understanding of how Mes think. But that's not gonna help us figure out where Meticulous is setting up the second elevator."

Hollywood gulped down a mouthful of trail mix. "Not without a Me tracker or something."

Motor almost choked on a bunch of M&M's. "That's it! We can track the new origami drive by using the old one!"

"I hate to burst your rare moment of confidence," said Resist, "but the old origami drive is broken at the bottom of an elevator shaft."

"But there should be enough life left in it for me to turn it into a transponder. I just need the right equipment. Uh, and somebody has to climb down the shaft to get the drive."

We all looked to Resist, but she'd already taken off for the elevator. She came back moments later with the origami drive in her hands and grease smudges on her skin.

"So where the fudge do we get the rest of the equipment you need, if you'll pardon my language?" said Hollywood.

Resist tossed the drive to Motor like a Frisbee, then broke into another granola bar. "Can't believe I'm saying this, but Hollywood has a point. Your Earth isn't as advanced as the ones we come from."

"Yeah, you don't even have holo-TV," Hollywood said.

"On behalf of my Earth, you can all get bent, thanks."

Motor called up pictures on his MePad, boxes with wires and antennas that looked familiar. "I just need a few simple pieces. But they're a little pricey. Mom's lab would have this stuff. It'll be all locked up for the night, though, so forget that."

Hollywood puffed out his chest. "I'm a master thief now. I can get it."

Resist rolled her eyes. "All you stole was a voice!"

"I know where I've seen this stuff!" I said. "And we wouldn't have to steal from Mom's lab."

"What do you have in mind?" asked Motor.

"How do you feel about dead animals in formaldehyde?"

★ 33 ★

No Place Like

It's not every day you see a set of quadruplets riding on a bus together, especially quadruplets as scuffed up and exhausted as us. We attracted more than our share of stares, lined up as we were along the back seat. But the other Mes hardly noticed as they bombarded me with questions about everything they saw on the streets rolling by.

Hollywood: "Why isn't every movie playing at that cinema about superheroes? On my Earth, *all* movies since the dawn of cinema have been about superheroes."

Motor: "Your Earth calls them salad bars? On mine they're called germ exchanges."

Resist: "People here are still burning gas, eating red meat, and using images of Santa to sell soda? Do we have time to get a protest going?"

I got so distracted trying to explain to them the con-
cept of video-game-watching videos (nobody on their
Earths had thought that up?!?) that I almost didn't notice
our stop. We got off and took the sneaky back way to the
side of the school, which turned out to be a good thing:
scads of students and parents were filing through the
front entrance.

"Oh, right, Student Showcase Night," I said from our
hiding spot behind a school bus in the parking lot.

The MeMinder piped up. "Student Showcase begins in
ten minutes."

I could only imagine where Mom and Dad were right
now. Riding around the town looking for me? I would have
texted them but my phone had died. Hopping between realities can be a huge battery drain.

Resist peered at the schedule on the sign outside the
school. "So remind me again why I've traveled across dozens of dimensions just to attend the science fair."

Hollywood read alongside her. "And don't forget the
basketball game and the sneak peek of the play."

Motor shook his head in surrender, which came so
naturally to him. "Let's just forget it. There's no way we'll
be able to rob Lunt's supply closet with all these people
around."

"There you go again, giving up too easy," said Resist.
"Obviously, we just need to find a different way in."

A minute later, we stood in the shadows just outside the
school's service entrance, where delivery trucks dropped
off the food-sludge they served in the cafeteria. It would

have been the perfect place to slip into the building unseen . . . if Click and Dare hadn't gotten there first. Dare wore my basketball uniform, while Click pranced around in Nash's Benedict Arnold costume, which was about three sizes too big for him. Seeing them dressed that way was like bolting awake from a nightmare. They were pretending to be me!

"Jiminy Cricket!" whispered Hollywood. "What are those two doing here?"

"Stealing my life!" I hissed.

"Hush!" said Resist. "They're arguing about something."

"I'm telling you, Nash will be with the cops for at least a few hours," said Dare.

Click twisted his fingers, anxious. "All our graffiti? The broken windows? The punctured tires? They'll never believe he did it."

"Sure they will," said Dare. "We tagged all those walls with 'Nash wuz here.' Just enjoy the moment. We've got no more equipment to steal. We've earned some Me time."

Click waved his hands in distress. His folded fingers looked like flesh pretzels. "Meticulous only told us to hold down the fort! He didn't say anything about getting so . . . involved!"

Dare made a fart sound with his lips, just like Resist had. I didn't find the connection cute. "Meticulous never said we *couldn't* do these things either. Even if we screw up out there, it's not like this is our Earth. We'll be long gone and never have to deal with the embarrassment."

Just the thought of these two performing as me in public made me barfy. I'd never live it down.

Click grinned. "Well, when you put it that way, how can I say no?"

He didn't smile for long, not once Resist leapt into action. She tackled them both at the same time, then had us tie them up with some bungee cords we'd found on the loading dock.

"Before you put us to the question, just know up front that we've been left in the dark about where Meticulous is." Dare spoke with the calm of a kid who's gotten in trouble more than once.

Click, on the other hand, was a nervous wreck. "Yeah, we swear! He sent us straight to Mom's lab to steal stuff as soon as we arrived! After we got it, Mobster picked it up. Then he told us to stick around and pretend to be Wild Me so nobody would notice he was gone. So we were actually doing you a favor!"

"Yeah, and by the way?" said Dare. "Your version of Mom can't cook!"

"You had dinner at my house?!" My brain liquefied at the thought of this Me eating with my parents. So I focused on the positive—at least somebody had shown up for dinner.

Hollywood started acting tough, like he was auditioning for a cop show. "Stop lying and tell us where Meticulous is!"

I put a hand on his shoulder. "No, they're telling the truth. They're not licking their lips, or scratching their arms, or doing any of those other things Mes do when we fib."

Hollywood rubbed at the last red splotch left on his face. "I never noticed we did any of that stuff, and it's my job to pay attention to body language. I'm an actor, after all."

"Yeah, but not a good actor," Dare said. Click giggled.

"That's enough out of you two," said Resist. She sealed their mouths with a roll of duct tape lying on the steps. Hollywood looked grateful.

"So, onward to Lunt's supply closet, then?" I said. "Time's ticking."

"Hold up," said Resist. "Motor, how long will it take for you to build your tracker?"

Motor groaned. "A while. And I have to do it here at school. The equipment's too delicate to move somewhere else."

"So we're stuck here for a bit," said Resist. "And if these two framed Nash for vandalism or whatever, Average really will have to fill in for him on the team. And in the play. On top of doing the science fair."

Hollywood slapped me on the back. "The show must go on."

"I can't do even one of those things!" I said. "How am I supposed to do all three?!"

"You won't have to," said Resist.

"Are you giving up already?" said Motor. "Isn't that my job?"

"I'm not giving up, and neither are you." Resist yanked the basketball uniform off Dare and pulled it over her shirt. "We're gonna finish what these losers started. Just one question: What's basketball?"

★ 34 ★

Show-Off

Greasy hot dog foil, sticky gum, soggy nacho cartons, and other trash rained all around me under the gym bleachers. But I couldn't complain. Beyond the trash that people up above tossed through the gaps in the seats, this was an unbeatable spot for somebody to watch a basketball game in secret. I had lots of room to stretch out and work on my science fair project, and I could see the court just fine between the legs of parents and kids. The only problem? I'd accidentally positioned myself below Mom and Dad. I might not have even noticed them at all if I hadn't seen Dad's *Lord of the Rings* socks right in front of me.

Mom's voice filtered down to me through the buzz of the crowd: "I hope Meade got his project done. He sure seemed odd at dinner. What was that he asked for? Chocolate chip spaghetti with prunes? I don't think he was joking either. And what was up with him refusing a ride from us to school?"

"Guess he had to get here early for all this stuff tonight," said Dad.

They went quiet, like they had nothing else to say to each other. Back in the day, they would have yammered away about work, movies, the *Dungeons & Dragons* podcast they used to do together, or most anything. Were they really headed for a divorce, like Meticulous had predicted? And what was Dare thinking, ordering some stupid dish from his stupid Earth?

Music blared and the crowd roared as my teammates ran onto the court one by one. The dung beetles and their anxiety balls stormed my stomach with a vengeance. So many parts of this plan could go wrong. Resist came from a world without ball-based sports and was about to start in a basketball game. Likewise, nobody had invented hip-hop on Hollywood's world, and he had less than an hour to memorize three rap songs. Meanwhile, Motor was on the verge of a panic attack back in Lunt's supply closet as he built some sort of tracker. I should have stayed to calm him down, but I had to see for myself how Resist and Hollywood did as me. They held my fate in their hands.

Strangely enough, the only thing I felt good about was my science fair project. In the end, it had actually been fun to make. The origami drive had inspired a much simpler idea I knew I could whip together from scratch in time. It wouldn't be A, or even C, material, but at least it was something to turn in.

When the announcer introduced "Meade Macon" and Resist ran out onto the court, worried whispers buzzed around the crowd. They must have been wondering where Nash was. But Mom had something else on her mind: "What did he do to his hair?"

Other parents seemed just as confused by Resist, and more than a few kids laughed at the sight of her. But they all shut up once they saw her play. As soon as the whistle blew, she got the ball, weaved around the other players, and scored in a matter of seconds. There was a moment of stunned silence, and then the crowd went nuts, whooping and cheering. Resist didn't slow down to bask in the glory. She played even better than Nash would have, stealing balls, zipping down the court, making basket after basket. She dominated the game, setting new school records in the first few minutes. Mom and Dad sat closer and closer together as they cheered her on. They even hugged each other after Resist sank her fifth three-pointer.

Much as I wanted to keep watching, I tore myself away and wrapped up my project. For a last-minute idea that had come to me out of sheer desperation, it could have turned out worse. Toward the end of the first half, I finished and snuck it out to the hallway with the other presentations. Mr. Lunt was busy talking to some parents, so I set up my display on the last empty table, then snuck back under the bleachers with no one the wiser.

Resist kept scoring right up until the blare of the half-time buzzer, at which point the team hoisted her in the air. I'd always wanted to get carried off by a grateful team, so it was like a dream come halfway true. I might have felt jealous if my guilt hadn't been so strong. It didn't feel right to get credit for work somebody else had done.

The cheers got so loud that Ms. Assan had to scream into the mic just to be heard. "You enjoyed Meade on the court, and now you get to see him and the rest of our wonderful drama class as we present a few scenes from our upcoming production of the hit musical *Benedict!*"

My chest went tight as Twig and the rest of the drama class poured into the gym, rapping about the Revolutionary War hero turned traitor. I'd been through dozens of practices and still forgot the lyrics, so how could Hollywood possibly know them? He missed his cue to enter the stage, and a big part of me hoped he'd simply bailed. But at the last minute, just before his solo, Hollywood surprised everybody with an entrance that wasn't in the script: he slid down from the ceiling on a climbing rope, belting out his lines in perfect rhythm with the beat. Mom, Dad, and the entire crowd screamed in ecstasy, like this was some sort of arena concert.

Hollywood only got better from there. As soon as his feet hit the court, he fell in with the background dancers, aping their moves step by step. His energy rubbed off on the other actors, who danced better than they ever had in practice. Twig especially put extra passion into her number "Oops,

We Picked the Wrong Side" and held her own with Hollywood during "Call Us Mr. and Mrs. Traitor." The two of them had what Ms. Assan would call chemistry. During the big finale, "Sorry, America, My Bad," Hollywood gave Twig a kiss that seemed to make her swoon for real, just like she did in all my daydreams.

But this wasn't a daydream. It was a nightmare. I was a liar and a cheat. I'd tricked Twig, Mom and Dad, and everyone else in the audience. Even worse, now I'd have to live up to these lies. From this point on, everybody would expect me to be a basketball pro and a theater star. The moment they saw the real me in action, they'd be severely disappointed.

When the lights came back on and the cast took their bows, Mom and Dad jumped from their seats to ignite a gym-wide standing ovation. The rest of the crowd followed their lead, and the applause went on forever. Hollywood tried to act humble and embarrassed, staggering backward as if blown away by the attention, but he clearly loved it. As he ran off the court with the rest of the cast, I could

 only hope he wouldn't linger backstage to soak up more praise. Resist had ordered us to meet at the loading dock right after the play.

Crawling to the far end of the bleachers, I popped out just a few steps from the exit. Everybody was so focused on talking about the fake me that they didn't notice the real one making a hasty departure. It would have been a nice clean getaway—if

Mom and Dad hadn't had a radar sense for finding me. They rushed up and hugged me before I even saw them coming.

Though I needed to ditch them something fierce, I took a moment to enjoy the attention. "Thanks for not being dead," I told them, getting a little choked up.

"What?" said Mom.

"Nothing."

"We loved how much you were enjoying yourself on the field!" said Dad, breaking off the hug.

"In basketball it's called a court, dear," Mom corrected. They both giggled. When was the last time those two had giggled together?

Twig announced herself with a punch to my arm. She made as if to hug me too, but I froze up. It didn't feel right, since I hadn't done anything hug-worthy. I couldn't even bear to go on with this lie any longer. I took a deep breath and geared up to confess everything to the people I loved the most on Earth Ninety-Nine.

That's when the speakers crackled and Mr. Lunt asked, "Is Meade Macon back on the court yet? Meade Macon?"

All eyes turned to me. A murmur of confusion spread through the auditorium. The audience must have wondered why I wasn't suiting up for the next half of the game. If they looked a little closer, they'd see how much my entire body shook from the sheer terror of being called out by a teacher who hated me. Had my project been so bad he had to complain about it in front of the entire school?

Mr. Lunt held up my poster, "Three-Dimensional Representations of Alternate Earths." "You know, when I first saw that Meade had submitted this project, I'll admit, I thought it sounded pretty bogus. But as I looked over the math he'd done and the precision he used to represent those equations through origami, I realized I was looking at one of the most creative science fair ideas I've seen in a long time. So this year, I want to give a special citation to acknowledge this achievement: 'Most Original' goes to Meade Macon!"

The crowd exploded yet again with shouts and applause, and this time it was all for me. The real me. Well, mostly. I'd actually just made up the equations, but they must have looked real enough to fool Lunt.

Mom and Dad screamed louder than they had for Resist or Hollywood, and Twig punched me in the arm harder than ever. Now, *this* was a dream come true.

Or it would have been a dream come true if the cops hadn't shown up at that moment to arrest me.

★ **35** ★

Caught on Camera

The local version of the cops who'd chased me on Earth One stood at the gym entrance, but this time I didn't have a scooter for a getaway. Nash appeared at their side and pointed straight at me. "That's him! He's the one who destroyed all that stuff around town, not me! He's the one in the videos!"

At the mention of videos, half the audience broke out their phones and started tapping away to see for themselves.

"What's all this about?" asked Mom and Dad.

Twig's phone pinged, and she clicked on a video someone had just sent her. Dare's voice came in loud and clear over the speaker: "Look at me, I'm Meade Macon! And I'm breaking this window just for the fun of it!" Crash!

With a sinking feeling, I realized Dare and Click had posted videos of themselves on their vandalism rampage.

Mom and Dad watched the video too, and each new wave of disappointment on their faces wiped away the glory I'd just gained. In seconds I went from hero to villain.

"Meade, what's the deal?" Twig might as well have been asking on behalf of the entire audience, who glared at me like I was a scumbag. I avoided Mom's and Dad's eyes completely.

Even if I knew where to start explaining, I'd never have time to finish, not with the cops closing in.

That's why, when the door opened a crack and three sets of carbon-copy hands wrapped around my arms to pull me through, I didn't protest one bit.

★ 36 ★

Like, Comment, Subscribe

It's not easy to watch irrefutable evidence of yourself committing crimes you didn't actually commit. But that's how I was forced to spend the bus ride to Meticulous's hideout, stewing as Motor played all six of Dare Me's vandalism videos on his MePad. The other Mes shared my disgust.

"They're doing all the stuff they know they can't get away with on their own Earths!" said Resist.

"They're making idiots of themselves on camera!" said Motor.

"Yeah," said Hollywood. "I mean, I make an idiot of myself on camera too, but at least I get paid for it!"

We'd bolted from school and lost the cops by sneaking between some dumpsters. We'd left Click and Dare there, bound and gagged with the trash. Then we'd hid at the bus stop to make sense of Motor's tracker. It had placed the new elevator somewhere in the warehouse district, but we couldn't pinpoint a location until Hollywood filled in the missing piece. "That's where the other Janus is, the Janus North! I did community theater there as a tyke, played the Lonely Wildebeest in *Zoo Animals on Wheels.*"

Google marked the hotel as "permanently closed," just like its twin downtown. In other words, if you needed to build a dimension-hopping elevator in private, you could have done a lot worse than this place.

When the bus pulled up to our exit, we stepped into an abandoned street free of people but full of shadows. The desolate office parks and creaky old warehouses looked downright haunted at night.

We watched the bus drive away, leaving us all alone in a dark and creepy wasteland. Hollywood darted his eyes around, clutching his chest like his heart might explode. "Everybody on the bus recognized us from the videos! I saw them make phone calls, probably to the night watch!"

"You mean the crime crushers?" Resist scanned the streets for any sign of trouble.

"Are you talking about the Be on Your Best Behavior or Else Patrol?" said Motor.

A siren wailed a few streets away. "Whatever you call them, they're coming!" I yelled.

A patrol car sped into the intersection and zoomed toward us, flashing its lights. As the rest of us froze,

Resist took off in a run—right for the cops. "I'll draw them away!"

Before any of us could argue, she jumped in front of the car. It screeched to a halt, and she charged to the left. I dragged Motor and Hollywood the opposite way, cutting through a gravel strip between two parking lots. The officers took the bait and chased after Resist.

I led the others through a cement graveyard for rusting old food trucks with names like Guac 'N Roll and Polenta to Go Around. From there we reached the Janus North in no time.

The hotel looked just as deserted as the one downtown. I had started to cross the street for the entrance when Motor pulled me back. "Not so fast!" He pointed to the SecureMe cameras mounted all around the building.

"Smile, you're on camera." Resist stepped out of the darkness. The other Mes and I jumped in unison, like we were doing a Zumba workout together.

"You okay?" I said. "Did you lose them?"

"For now. Wait here a second." She ran around the block in record time, careful to stay in the shadows. When she got back a minute later, her face looked grim. "No way can we sneak in without being seen on camera. Motor, can you hack the security system?"

With a queasy face, Motor broke out a MePad and tapped

away. "Nah, it's too sophisticated. Troll must have put it in place. I can't match his skills."

"You can't or you're too much of a wuss to try?" said Resist.

Motor threw up his hands just like all of us had done at some point or another that day. "One wrong move and I'd set off an alarm!"

Hollywood butted in. "There was this one *Baker's Dozen* episode where we broke into the town library to delete my character's overdue-book fine. We caused a distraction with some smoke bombs and fart spray."

I figured Resist would just tell Hollywood to shut up. Instead: "That's actually a good idea!"

Hollywood went from stunned to stoked. "Awesome! Then all we need is some smoke bombs and fart spray!"

"I have a less moronic distraction in mind," said Resist. "Motor, instead of shutting down the alarms, can you set them off? I want it to look like we're breaking into the back entrance."

Motor brightened. "Not a problem!" He tapped at the MePad some more. "Ready when you are." He held his finger over the Enter key on the screen.

Resist crouched down and motioned for the rest of us to do the same. "If I'm lucky, the losers in there will be too busy focusing on the back to see me coming from the front. You all stay here. I'll see you again once I've taken down Meticulous."

"What?!" I said. "No way! We're in this together!"

Resist shook her head. "None of you are ready. Motor, you have no confidence. Average, you can't control your weird powers. Hollywood, well, you're Hollywood."

Hollywood looked more relieved than offended. "Fair enough."

Resist grabbed Motor's MePad and pressed the Enter key. A muffled buzz echoed from the rear of the building. With that, Resist sprinted to the front entrance, leaving us behind.

I didn't hesitate to set off after her, and neither did Motor, though he took longer. Hollywood came last, and probably only because he was scared to be left alone.

Resist shot us an especially nasty glare as we crowded beside her on either side of the doors. I had a stirring speech ready about how this was our fight just as much as hers, but she raised a finger to her lips. Together, we peeked in through the plate-glass windows.

The most dangerous Mes of Me Con had set up shop in the lobby, and they weren't getting along. Troll typed madly on a laptop at the check-in counter, screaming at Ren Faire, who screamed at Mobster, who screamed back at both of them as he stormed out of the room. His exit gave Troll and Ren Faire more space to shout at each other.

"Sakes alive, if you'll pardon the expression," whispered Hollywood. "Your trick with the alarm worked!"

"Time to take advantage of it." And with no other warning, Resist jumped up, kicked open the door, and rushed in.

We followed right behind her, which at this point was getting to be a habit.

★ 37 ★

Don't Tread on Me

By the time the rest of us burst into the lobby, Resist had already tackled Ren Faire. He and Troll hadn't even seen her coming.

Before we could do anything to help, Mobster rushed back into the room. The massive Me yanked Resist off Ren Faire and pinned her to the floor. "Nice try, pretty princess!"

Standing up, Ren Faire drew his sword and pointed it at me. "Prithee, where art the rest of thee?!"

Still at his keyboard, Troll toggled through different camera views of the empty halls on the monitor. "It's just them and nobody else. The alarm was only a diversion. Can't believe I fell for Motor's hack! I'm alerting Meticulous!"

Hollywood knelt in front of Ren Faire. "Hear me out first! They forced me to do this! I didn't want to! Please! I have information for Meticulous! All about their plans!"

I couldn't believe it. After all we'd been through, how could Hollywood turn traitor like that? "Oh, come on!" I said. "We don't have *plans*!"

"Don't play dumb!" Actual tears streamed down Hollywood's face. "You rigged the hotel to blow up!"

It took me a second to catch on and another second to play along. "Quiet! You'll ruin everything!" I hoped I sounded convincing.

"It's too late!" Resist wheezed from beneath Mobster's full nelson. "He's given our plans away!" She sold the line like a pro.

Motor said nothing, which was just as well, since he looked ready to laugh.

Troll threw up his hands in that frustrated Me way, an unwelcome reminder that he was one of us. "This is a lie! They can't have put bombs around the building!"

"Yes, they did!" said Hollywood, squeezing out a few extra sobs. "They got them from Dynamite Me!"

"I hath never heard of this Dynamite Me!" said Ren Faire.

Hollywood didn't miss a beat. "Had you ever heard of Wild Me until today? I tell you, he'll do anything to get his way! Even kill us all!" He broke down all over again in a new burst of weeping.

Ren Faire looked disgusted. "Thou must be telling the truth. Thou art not a good enough actor to fake a cry like this. Get up, knave, and dry thy unseemly tears."

Still blubbering, Hollywood struggled to stand, or pretended to. When Ren Faire stepped closer to help him up, Hollywood struck, kicking Ren Faire's legs out from under him. The Me crumpled to the floor in a rattle of leather and metal.

"And that's how we did it on *Pallin' with the Shaolin*!" said Hollywood. "Bet they don't teach you that at Shakespeare school!"

Ren Faire didn't even have time to shout a Shakespearean curse word before Hollywood fell on him. Resist seized on the distraction to push Mobster off herself and flip back on her feet.

The sight of Hollywood and Resist going toe to toe with their least favorite Mes was all the encouragement Motor needed to take on Troll. In moments the two were locked in a tug-of-war for Troll's laptop. I rushed over to help, but Motor waved me away. "Go find Meticulous!"

"Yeah, we'll hold them off!" said Hollywood, yanking Ren Faire's armor and undertunic up over his face.

I looked to Resist as she wrestled with Mobster. She nodded back in a *You got this* sort of way.

So I ran to the elevator bank for the fight that had probably been inevitable from the moment I read that first note from another world. It was time for a showdown between Meticulous Me and his archrival. The thorn in his side. The bane of his existence.

Average Me.

★ **38** ★

Meticulous Me

Meticulous was so focused on fixing up his new elevator that he didn't seem to notice the half dozen duplicates of himself duking it out in the next room. Or maybe he just didn't care.

The new control panel he fussed over looked nothing like the hundred-button original. This rendition was much smaller, with a number keypad and a green digital display screen. Somehow it seemed both simpler and far more sinister.

"Why, hullo, mate." He didn't look up from his work. "Such a pleasant surprise!"

"Yeah, and such a welcome home! I just loved having those idiots you brought here ruin my life."

Meticulous grinned as he plugged in the last loose wire. "You did a number on my world too. The Me Corp. board of directors had a lot of questions about why the police reported someone who looked just like me doing a bunk on them all over town."

"That's nothing compared to robbery, vandalism, and whatever else the cops are after me for now. Plus, the evidence is all over the internet."

Meticulous put the panel in place and started screwing it in. "My assistants have kept busy, haven't they?"

I had to change the subject before I lost what little cool I had left. "So, this is your new elevator?"

Meticulous tightened the final screw and admired his work. "Lush, isn't she?"

"What's so different with this one?"

Meticulous placed the screwdriver back in his tool kit with the fussy care of a florist arranging flowers. He tapped a button on the keypad, and a burning green light blazed behind it. "I'm sure you've figured out how the origami drive works, or you wouldn't be here."

"It folds the barrier between universes to get you from one Earth to another."

He beamed at me like I was a dog who'd just done a trick the right way. "Brilliant! And trust me when I say that finding those folds isn't bloody easy. Took me forever to figure out the first hundred Earths. It's been a few years now, and

I only just found a way to get to Earth Ninety-Nine. I mean, folding an origami polar bear is hard enough, but an octopus? You, however, seem to have an innate gift for it. Those origami you made for me matched my calculations down to the millimeter."

"Calculations? So then it *is* geometry, just like Motor guessed."

Meticulous gave me one of his signature smug looks. "Dumb luck, I'm sure. But it's true that the folds come from loads of complicated calculations. They only happen to look like animals and other tosh. It's our minds that see a pattern in the randomness."

"There's nothing random about an Atlantic pygmy octopus. You know how long it took me to figure out how to do one of those?"

Meticulous stooped down to line up the tool kit with the elevator wall. "That's why I needed you and your precision. Your folds are cracking. It's as if the multiverse itself told you the exact measurements I needed."

"I doubt that." Though I'd suspected the very same thing. "I've just had a lot of practice."

"It's more than that. After all, you were raised here on Earth Ninety-Nine."

"What's so special about here?"

"Isn't it obvious? It's an Interdimensional Roundabout."

"What's that?"

"Like it sounds! An Interdimensional Roundabout acts as a hub between all dimensions. The barrier blocking out other Earths is weaker in a place like this, more porous.

Being raised here all your life has given you a unique connection to the multiverse. That's why you understand how to work the origami drive, even though you can't even begin to grasp the math behind it."

I thought about how I'd felt on Earth Zero under the Rip, and later, when I'd touched the energy in the origami drive. My "connection to the multiverse" would explain all the weird stuff going on in my brain and body since I got that first note. Still, I hated to admit that Meticulous might be right about anything. "Whatever" was all I could think to say.

"I'd theorized the existence of an Interdimensional Roundabout, but I didn't think I'd ever find one. Blimey, I'd thought ninety-nine worlds would be it for me and the elevator. But then I learned how you, the most dull-as-dishwater Me I'd ever met, had been to my Earth, overriding the controls I'd put in place to prevent that very thing from happening. That's when I suspected your Earth was special. And I was right! By making an elevator here, I can now reach countless worlds!"

"But is it worth the risk? Remember what happened to your elevator the first time around? The way you made the Rip?"

Meticulous shoved a finger in my face. "That's a load of codswallop! I didn't bloody well know that would happen! And besides, nobody got hurt! If anything, I made Earth Zero a more interesting place!"

Every nerve in my body wanted to reach out and shake

224

some sense into him, but Mom, Dad, and Twig were counting on me to keep it together. So was all of Earth Ninety-Nine. Plus a hundred other dimensions, for that matter. "But what if it happens again?"

Meticulous brushed imaginary dust off his jacket, acting cool and collected again. "This new elevator won't have those unfortunate side effects."

"How can you be so sure?"

"Because, unlike other Mes, I learn from my bloomers. For instance, I don't intend to let you slip away again. Once that little kerfuffle's over in the next room, my assistants will find a place to keep you safe and locked up. Juvenile Hall, perhaps? You could make new folds for me from your cell. It would be rubbish not to make use of your talent."

"No way! I'm not helping you anymore! And I'm not going anywhere!"

"I thought you might feel that way. But don't worry, I've set aside the next few minutes on my schedule to persuade you."

And with no warning, Meticulous lunged for me.

★ 39 ★

All of Me

Meticulous tried to punch me, but I blocked him with reflexes I had no right to possess. The fizz was back. If I could just control it this time, I might have a fighting chance.

"I knew it!" said Meticulous, more excited than I'd ever seen him. "That really takes the biscuit! You just channeled Resist and her fighting skills!"

I tried to shove Meticulous to the floor, but he spun just out of reach, moving faster than anybody in knickers and a cravat should have been able to. He twirled behind me and clocked me in the back of the head. "I got that move from Bollywood Musical Me," he said. "Took me long enough to learn it."

I backed away. "What are you talking about?!"

He crept toward me. "I've worked very hard to learn the skills and gain the knowledge of every Me. You, on the other hand, have had them handed to you like a cheat sheet. Been able to run faster than usual? You can thank Marathon Me for that. Picked any locks lately? That was you stealing Escape Me's trick. The way you kicked Motor's cart across the floor? Ultimate Mixed Martial Arts Me. Any special new abilities you think are 'superpowers' actually came from another Me. You're not All of Me. You're just a cheap knock-off."

Trash talk is even worse when it's true. Being called a knock-off cut deep and left me too stunned to avoid his choke hold. I couldn't break free of his tightening arm, but my fizzing body figured out a work-around. Shifting my weight, I flipped him over my shoulder.

The move would have been a lot more satisfying if Meticulous hadn't managed to land on his feet. He twisted around to face me. "We both did a Rodeo Clown Me acrobatic move just then. The difference is you weren't even aware you were doing it."

He came at me with a dropkick to my gut that I barely blocked before striking back.

As the two of us traded blow after blow, Meticulous called out the Mes whose abilities we aped together: "Lucha Libre Wrestling Me!" "Whirling Dervish Me!" "Aqua

Aerobics Me!" After he pounded me in the ribs with his knee, my body flooded with the strength of Mobster Me, and I brought him down.

Meticulous smiled up at me as he wriggled to break free. "You want to know my theory?"

"Nah, I'm good. I'll pass."

He kept talking anyway. "My theory is you were exposed to one of Mum's portals in the womb, seeing as how her experiment worked here."

Mom's experiment worked here? Wrapping my head around that thought, I let my grip slip an inch. That was just enough room for Meticulous to free one of his arms and grasp a tender spot between my neck and shoulder. He squeezed until all my limbs locked up. I was paralyzed.

"This nerve pinch comes courtesy of Acupuncture Me. You know, the New Agey one with the man bun, who everybody makes fun of?" Meticulous stood up. "Did you know he could do that? No? Guess you should have gone to his workshop."

All I could do was lie there on my side as Meticulous looked down at me and shook his head. "So many Mes to mimic, and you still lost. You know why? Because you didn't work and train to get those skills like I did. There's nothing you can do that I can't do better. Not to crow, but I truly am the best of all the Mes. If there really was an All of Me, I'd be it."

He nudged me with his foot and I fell over, landing right on my pinched shoulder. The impact knocked something loose inside me, and my fingers started twitching. I could tell my arms and legs would work again too, with enough time. But time was the thing I didn't have.

Meticulous stepped into the elevator, running a loving hand over the control panel. Maybe if I stalled for a while, I could get enough movement back in my body to stop him.

"You talk like Mom's experiment succeeded here, but that's bull. It didn't work. She totally bombed in front of all those other professors."

"Or so everyone thought. Interdimensional travel is a completely new science. No one at that conference knew how to detect a portal, including your mum. She opened a portal, all right; she just didn't know it. It was probably no bigger than a pinprick and lasted only a millisecond, but she did it."

"And that's what made Earth Ninety-Nine an 'Interdimensional Roundabout'?"

Meticulous grunted with impatience. "That, and her second experiment here at the Janus North.

"The portals she made here sent out . . . you could call them echoes. Echoes to the Janus Hotels in other realities, where other editions of her never got it right. I built my first elevator on one of those echoes, but it was too faint. Now you could say I've gone straight to the source. And the results should be brilliant."

"Wait, if everything started here, with that first experiment, wouldn't that make this place Earth One?"

"Hey, I built the elevator, so I get to do the naming." He

waved his hand toward the lobby. "No sense waiting on the fight to end out there. It's time to leave this corner of the multiverse for good."

"But this thing might blow everything up! It'll be Earth Zero all over again!"

He fluffed the lace spilling from his jacket sleeve. "It's worth the risk. Oh, don't look at me like that.  Face it, you and the blokes here simply aren't as real to me as the people of my Earth. What happens to you isn't important in the end."

My arms worked just enough to push myself up. "You don't mean that. I know you. I know us. We're the same person deep down."

I'd seen Meticulous cycle through calm, angry, majorly angry, and excited in the span of a few minutes. Now he just looked sad. "Ninety-eight worlds between us. We're nothing alike."

He lifted a finger to press the keypad, but he never got to touch it. A huge arm, too big to be a Me's, reached in and grabbed Meticulous by the shoulder, yanking him out of the car. "Not so fast, you little punk!"

It was Nash. The Nash of my world. And he was done playing nice.

★ 40 ★

Help Me Out

No matter how smart he was, no matter how much training he'd done, no matter how long he'd tamed the Nash of
his Earth, Meticulous came hardwired with the deep fear
of this monster that was built into all of us. That's why the
most accomplished, most able, most all-around superior Me
of a hundred Earths went limp as Nash pulled him from the
elevator and pinned him against the opposite wall. It was
equal parts satisfying and scary to watch.

"The cops are looking for you!" Nash snarled. "Thing is,
I found you first!"

Meticulous squirmed in his grip but couldn't get free.
"H-how did you find me?"

"Stop talking in that dumb accent!" said Nash. "I saw

what bus you got on and followed it. Walked around until I noticed those kids fighting in the window. Who are they, anyway? It's creepy how much you all look alike." He squinted at me. "Especially that one. Are you cousins or something?"

"Uh, right, yes, we all are," said Meticulous. "It's a family squabble."

Nash leaned into Meticulous. "I *should* beat you to a pulp after what you did to me. But I guess handing you over to the cops will just have to do."

This would have been a good time for me to get up, but my body was a deflated whoopee cushion. I wouldn't be moving for a while. Nash had just started to peel Meticulous off the wall when Twig ran into the elevator bank. She looked like she'd been through a haunted house. "Those kids up front, they look exactly like . . ." She trailed off as her eyes went from me to Meticulous and back again.

"Twig, it's dangerous here!" said Nash. "You should wait by the bikes like we talked about!"

Jealousy surged through me. Since when were these two friendly enough to hunt me down together on bikes?

"What's going on?!" Twig directed the question at me, not at Nash, which was some small comfort, at least.

Nash squinted at me again, then at Meticulous. "You're not cousins. You're twins!"

The moment Nash looked back at me, Meticulous squeezed his shoulder. His body went rigid, and he thunked to the floor, as frozen as I'd been moments before. Twig wasted no time with shock or confusion. She rushed up to

Meticulous and kicked him in what the British would have called the goolies. He doubled over in pain.

Just then, with no warning, the MeMinder came to life on my wrist. "You have been sedentary for five minutes." I was about to use what little movement I'd gotten back in my arms to bash the thing to bits. Then I got a better idea. Something else in my reach needed a good bashing even more.

I had enough movement back in my arms to drag myself to the elevator controls. Reaching into the tool kit on the floor, I snatched up the screwdriver and rammed it into the keypad. It burst apart in a cloud of smoke and sparks.

"No!" screamed Meticulous. Twig tried to take him down again, but he got his death grip on her first. She collapsed beside Nash, paralyzed like the rest of us.

Meticulous rushed over to the elevator and picked up the broken keypad, all his calm melting away. If I'd ever wondered what I'd look like full-on, no-holds-barred angry, now I knew.

"Do you have any idea how much work I put into this?!" he screamed. "All those folds for new worlds I programmed into the origami drive! They're all lost now!"

"You mean *my* folds! *I* did all the work!" I didn't actually have a point beyond that—I just felt like I had to shout about something too.

Meticulous went from mad to happy in a split second. "Yes! That's it! You did all the work!" He ripped the panel cover off the wall with a yank. Behind it lay a thinner version of the origami drive. Green energy crackled inside the sleek and shiny ring. Origami Drive 2.0.

Meticulous grabbed me by the collar. "We're going to do this manually. I'll tell you what shape to fold, and you'll fold it."

"And what if I refuse?"

He gestured at the frozen bodies of Twig and Nash. Then he ran his finger across his throat. The invisible line he traced was very straight, very precise, and very Meticulous.

★ 41 ★

All About Me

I had no idea if Meticulous would actually hurt Twig and Nash more than he had already, but I didn't plan on finding out. "Okay, I'll do it."

The truth is, I couldn't have fought back anyway. I still couldn't stand up on my own, and my channeling trick seemed to have burned itself out in me. No more fizz. No more All of Me.

"Okay, then." Meticulous checked his MePad. "Start with an anglerfish. For Earth One Hundred Fourteen."

As soon as I started folding the energy, a big chunk of my anxiety fell away. Origami always cleared my head like that. If it weren't for Meticulous hovering around, I might have even enjoyed myself.

"So, what's your deal, exactly?" I said, shaping the light into a fish body. "Why's it so important for you to go 'deeper' into the multiverse?"

Not taking his eyes off my hands, Meticulous shrugged. "You know, curiosity and all that tosh."

"You can't lie to a Me. Not this Me, at least."

Meticulous checked the length of his fingernails. "Well, if you must know. Based on my calculations, this new list of Earths I've gathered should have the tech I've been seeking: the next generation of spacecraft, life-extension treatments, and artificial intelligence. I plan to bring these gewgaws to my world."

The truth hit me like Twig's kick to the groin. "You've done this before, haven't you?! You stole ideas from other worlds and passed them off as your own! The Missing Mes invented self-driving cars and smart toilets and all that other Me Corp. junk you've been selling on Earth One! You stole it from them to build Me Corp.!"

If being called a thief and a cheat hurt Meticulous's feelings, he didn't show it. "Back to folding now. You don't want to break your momentum."

Folding was the last thing I planned on doing just then. "Me Con was a scam all along! It was just a way for you to keep the Mes occupied so you could sneak into their worlds and steal ideas for your company! That was the real point of interviewing everybody, to see what tech they had back home! Tech you could steal!"

Lips tight, Meticulous wagged his thumb at Twig and

Nash. I took the hint and got back to the fish, but I didn't shut up. "And now that you've taken all the worthwhile ideas from a hundred worlds, you're all washed up. Which is why you need new worlds to rob."

Meticulous whipped a handkerchief from his breast pocket and shook it out a lot harder than he needed to. "And what's the harm, really?"

"The harm? Your greed and general butt-headedness have stranded everybody at Me Con! Wait a minute, I just realized: You didn't *banish* the Missing Mes. Your stupid, unstable elevator messed up their Earths, didn't it?!"

Meticulous buffed the already spotless wall around the origami drive. "Their Earths are fine. It's the portals to their Earths that may require some tweaking."

"So you went to their worlds to steal ideas too many times, and it wrecked their only way home?!"

"Like I said, I'll return them to their homes with this new and improved elevator. Eventually."

I was so mad I almost squished the fish head I'd just folded. "Was it worth it? Robbing them of their homes just to make a fast buck?"

Meticulous polished the wall hard enough to rub a hole through it. "That's tosh! This isn't about money, it's about Me Corp. and what it represents. It's about a Me actually doing something with his life. Do you know how bloody hard it was to build up the company?"

"Couldn't have been too hard if Dad started it for you."

"That failure? Pillocks! Not likely! It wasn't until I made some simple improvements to the MeMinder that Dad's naff little business took off."

"And from there you stole the MePads and MeCars and MeToilets?"

Meticulous wiped so hard the wall squeaked under his handkerchief. "It's not as if Dad could have ever thought up a single one of those products!"

"It's not like you did either. You didn't even invent the origami drive. Mom did!"

He threw the handkerchief on the floor and stomped on it with his boot. "It was just notes when I found it! Notes with the numbers all squiffy! Unlike *your* mum, *my* mum only got it one percent right. I did the other ninety-nine! Me!"

He trailed off, and his eyes went watery. Even his tears were neat and tidy, rolling down his cheeks in an orderly little stream.

"Your mom's dead," I said. "Is this about her or something?"

He choked back a sob. "What, you think I'm scouring the multiverse, trying to find a replacement for her? I'm not. I'm not happy she died, but I've moved on."

"Yeah, moved on to stealing stuff from the Mes."

Meticulous snatched up the handkerchief and shoved it into his pocket. "I made the origami drive! What else did I need to do?! Once I had the elevator up and running, I had a whole multiverse of brilliant new gadgets and inventions to choose from."

"But they aren't your ideas!"

"Rubbish! Anybody can invent a MePad or a MeLoo. I created from scratch a machine to travel between realities! After you've done that, you don't need to bloody well tinker around with anything else, because everything you need is already out there for the taking. It saves time, and time is crucial when you're a thirteen-year-old CEO!"

"What's your rush? You've got decades of being a CEO ahead of you."

He snorted. "I run Me Corp., but I could be sacked by the board of directors at any time. As it is, they're less than chuffed to have a kid at the head of a multibillion-dollar company. They only accept me as long as I roll out new doofers and upgrade the old ones every fiscal quarter. Do you know how much pressure that is?!" He took a deep breath to calm himself. "Now get back to work."

It was a good thing my hands were occupied with folding, because otherwise I'd have used them to strangle Meticulous. By pouring my frustration into the origami, I had it finished in no time. As soon as I put the final folds on the fins, the anglerfish started spinning.

It was time to visit a new Earth.

★ 42 ★

Flooded

My mind paid a visit to the next Earth before the elevator did.

With no warning, a vision flashed in my brain of a vast sea with buildings poking out of the water. A flooded city. Somehow I knew it wasn't just a hallucination. This was a sneak peek at Earth One Hundred Fourteen, where we were going next. I shook my head until the image cleared, telling myself it was just the exhaustion setting in.

"Let's go!" yelled Meticulous. The door rolled shut, and the elevator shot upward. I closed my eyes, bracing for an explosion. Nothing happened. The car kept moving.

Meticulous smiled as he adjusted his ruffles. "There, see? No boom. The new origami drive leaves no trace when

240

it crosses the dimensions. Your reality is safe, and all the other new realities we can reach now will be too. If my theory's right, this lovely will take us anywhere, even Earths that don't have a Janus or an elevator. It can open a portal on the most backward Earth, not that we'd ever want to go there!"

"Cool. So let's take this fancy new ride back to Me Con. If it works like you say, we could rescue the Mes and get them back home pronto."

Meticulous scrolled through his MePad. "Right now I have more important things to do."

"More important than saving your fellow Mes!? The Mes you left stuck there?!"

"As a matter of fact, yes!"

And with that, the elevator stopped, the doors opened, and a tidal wave of water rushed in.

"Close it!" shouted Meticulous as the deluge backed him into the wall.

I jabbed at the Close button, which hadn't been damaged when I busted the keypad. The doors shut, leaving several inches of water at the bottom of the car. Now it looked like a kiddy pool filled with murky seawater.

"What was that?!" I asked. Though deep down I knew. We'd reached an Earth covered in water, just like my vision. My brain really had seen where we were going ahead of time. Was this my "connection" to the multiverse at work? More important, could I do it again? But even if I got a sneak peek at our next destination, it wasn't like I had any say in where we went. What good did this strange new power really do me?

Meticulous fished his soggy tool kit from the water and pulled out a drone. A MeDrone, naturally. "Better scout around. Get ready to open the door again on my signal."

"Are you crazy?"

"Are you in a position to argue?"

Meticulous tapped the screen of his MePad, and the drone came to life, hovering in the air near his head. "Okay, do it."

Bracing myself, I pressed the Open button. Meticulous swiped at the screen, and the drone buzzed through the parting door as the water rushed in. "Now close it!" he yelled. But I was already one step ahead of him. The door shut, trapping more water inside with us. I still couldn't stand, so now the flood came up to my chest. It sloshed just a few feet below the origami drive and nearly reached Meticulous's knees.

Soaked from his knickers to his feet, Meticulous ignored the wet as he gazed at the view from the drone camera. He clenched the MePad so hard it made a popping sound. "It's a drowned world! I factored some climate change into my number-crunching, but not as much as I should have! This makes rubbish of my whole algorithm! That means the other worlds I mapped out are barmy too! Open the door! I need my drone back!"

I pressed Open, and another wave gushed in. Meticulous caught the drone just as I shut the doors. "It doesn't seem right to leave an Earth in that condition," I said. "Maybe we could help."

Meticulous tapped at the MePad like a viper striking prey. "The multiverse is a cruel place, and I've got bigger problems than a flooded world."

"Then what about our flooded elevator?" I said, shaking the water from my hands.

Meticulous didn't look up from the screen. "We'll dump the water out at the next stop. Right now I've got to recalculate all these bits and bobs! It may take hours!"

I sat in the stink and seaweed of my salty ocean bath, feeling exhaustion set in. All this folding and world-hopping was wearing out my head as well as my hands. My eyelids fluttered and my brain went hazy. Then Meticulous pounded his fist against the wall, jolting me awake. "This is a load of cack! I can't do the math in these conditions!"

I yawned. "Must be a lot of factors and stuff to keep track of."

Meticulous scoffed. "You don't even know the half of it! If you understood one percent of the math that went into this data, they'd herald you as a genius on your primitive little world."

Primitive? Who was he calling primitive? I was about to tell him off when my brain fizzed again, flashing on another world. I had a vision of a different Earth, one unlike any I'd heard about at Me Con. The fold for this world came into my head too, and with it, a plan for what to do when we got there. If I could pull it off, this was a chance—maybe my only chance—to stop Meticulous for good. The trick would be convincing him to take a little detour.

As ideas went, it was crazy, half formed, and more than likely disastrous. But if I'd learned anything, it was that crazy, half-formed, and more-than-likely-disastrous ideas were my specialty.

★ **43** ★

Survival of the Fittest

I chose my words carefully, so it was annoying when Meticulous ignored them. He didn't even look up from his MePad until I raised my voice to repeat what I'd just said: "What if it's not the calculations that are off, but the fact that you're calculating in the first place? Maybe crunching numbers isn't the way to do this."

That got his attention. "Absolute rubbish! I had to create an entirely new system of math to calculate the locations of any given parallel Earth! You're saying that was some kind of faff?!"

"Yeah, I am." Though in truth I didn't know what *faff* or any of his other Earth One Briticisms meant. "Think about it. Every fold you've come up with for the origami drive has a recognizable shape, right?"

He made an extravagant sigh to let me know how bored he was with this conversation. "As I told you before, the shapes are just a coincidence. They only happen to correspond with the numbers. Nothing more than pattern recognition. A trick of the mind."

"I don't think it's that simple. Maybe if we get the right shape, we'll get the right Earth too."

"That's bloody daft! The folds are just random blobs!"

"Are they? Of the folds you made to reach the original hundred Earths, how many looked like random blobs with no shape?"

He said nothing.

"That's what I thought," I said.

"Okay, so if what you're saying is even remotely true, how could we possibly predict what shapes to try?"

Here's where I had to be careful. "You said I had a connection to the multiverse, right? Well, maybe with your expert guidance, I could tap into that. Let's try an experiment. Name an origami shape for one of the first hundred Earths, and I'll guess the Me who goes with it."

Meticulous rolled his eyes. "Okay. How about a northern spitting spider?"

My mind fizzed, and the answer came to me gift-wrapped with a bow. "Earth Thirty-Four. Hollywood Me's world."

Meticulous hardly even tried to hide his surprise. "How did you guess?"

"I didn't. The multiverse told me. Go on, try another."

"Okay, then. How about a Pacific banana slug?"

Another name buzzed into my head. "That's easy. Mobster Me. Which is fitting, since he's got the mind of a slug."

Meticulous stared at me hard. "You're like the village idiot who's an unexpected genius at conkers."

"No idea what conkers is, but thanks."

"Come on, do you really think just folding some animal shape will get us to the Earth I need?"

"I think it's worth a try. Otherwise we could be here all week."

Meticulous threw up his hands in that familiar Me way. "Then by all means, be my guest. But I'm warning you, no dodgy business. I'm watching you, okay?"

"Whatever." I reached into the origami drive and took hold of the energy again. At this point the stuff felt like Silly Putty left out in the sun too long. Maybe the origami drive needed a break as much as I did.

"Wait," said Meticulous. "What shape are you even considering?!"

I forced my aching fingers to make the first folds. Though my hands wanted to fall right off, I managed to tease the energy into a body. "You want an Earth with spaceships and life extension and AI, right?"

"Well, any one of those would do for now."

"If this works, I can deliver all three in one go." I gave

the origami a few final touches, then waved my throbbing hands with a flourish. *"Voilà!"*

"A crane?"

"Hey, I don't make the shapes. The multiverse does."

Meticulous arched an eyebrow, but the elevator started moving before he could protest more than that.

"And anyway, what's the harm?" I added. "Whether this works out or not, at least we'll have a chance to drain the water at our next stop."

"We take a gander when we arrive, and if it doesn't work, we do things my way again. Math!"

Meticulous played it cool, but you didn't have to be a Me to recognize the greedy excitement written all over his face. He positioned himself at our next stop in front of the door, drone hovering beside him. He stared straight ahead, all his attention on the elevator door and the wonders it would show him when it opened. That's why he didn't notice me as I struggled back to my feet and waded through the water to stand behind him.

The moment the door opened, searing-hot air slapped our faces. Our ears roared with the buzz of a kajillion insects. Our noses filled with a stink stronger than a litter box for lions. We stood before a rain forest of vine-choked trees lit up by the brightest night sky I'd ever seen. The moon was huge, and there was no end to the stars around it. This was the biggest dose of raw nature I'd ever experienced. We'd reached the sort of "primitive Earth" Meticulous liked to pooh-pooh. No Janus, no city, no civilization.

Unless you counted the hairy, unwashed people in animal skins drinking water from the pond a few feet ahead of us.

Honest-to-goodness cave dwellers.

Nothing I'd seen about prehistoric people, from museum exhibits to cartoons, could have prepared me for them in real life. They weren't big and beefy—more like short and skinny. They didn't growl or even grimace at us, just stared in slack-jawed surprise, tilting their heads from side to side like bewildered house pets staring at a TV screen. The sight of a random magic box appearing out of nowhere with twins inside and lots of water spilling out confused them, but not in an angry way.

Meticulous hopped up and down in a panic. "Close the door!"

Which was when I tickled him in that certain spot of the neck. Like I'd hoped, he couldn't resist it any better than Hollywood had. As he jerked away, his body off balance, I planted my foot on his backside and kicked him into Earth Three Hundred Seventy-Six.

Before Meticulous even hit the ground, I hit the Close button, but the door wasn't fast enough. Meticulous regained his footing the second he touched soil and pivoted back toward the elevator, launching himself at the closing door. Just when it looked like he'd make it back in time, he tripped over a caveman who'd been napping in a clump of reeds.

Meticulous fell on his face right in front of me. Before

the door shut, I saw the napping caveman sit up with a grunt.

I only got the briefest glimpse of him, but I could have sworn under all the grime that he was a Me.

Caveman Me.

★ 44 ★

Earth in the Imbalance

I came back to Earth Ninety-Nine to find that the losers of Me Con had beaten the cool kids.

Hollywood, Motor, and Resist were tying up the Viral Mes with hotel bedding in the elevator bank. They'd even captured Click and Dare, who'd followed the bus to the hotel like Nash, only to get their butts whipped when they joined in the fight. They and everybody else in the room looked pretty dinged up, but my friends were the ones still standing.

That's right, I called them friends. We may have been four vastly different reproductions of the same person, but only friends would stick together through a mess like the one we'd just survived.

"Well, if it isn't All of Me!" said Hollywood. I raised my palm for a high five, but he brushed it aside and gave me a hug instead. I hugged right back, and Motor joined in too. When Hollywood waved Resist over, she pretended to tighten the pillowcase gags on the Virals.

"Oh, come on!" Hollywood told her. "Think of it as a huddle!"

Looking like she'd bitten into a rotten Bowel Blocker, Resist came over to pat us on the back a few times.

"You guys did it!" I said.

"No, *you* did it!" said Motor.

"And what exactly did you do?" asked Hollywood.

"Long story." I broke off the hug when I noticed Twig and Nash in the doorway to the lobby. Back on their feet, they watched the four of us like we might sprout fangs at any moment. They stood close together, but more in a scared way than a romantic way, at least where Twig was concerned. When Nash tried to hold Twig's hand, she slapped it aside.

"You guys okay?" I asked them.

They both nodded, dazed.

"You're the real one, right?" Nash asked me. "I mean, the one from, uh, here?"

"Yeah, it's me."

Nash looked thoughtful. "The vandalism. The call to the cops about me. The prank with the homework. That was the other Meades who did that?"

"I know it's hard to take in, but yeah. Thanks for showing up when you did to stop Meticulous. Um, even if you thought he was me."

Everybody tensed up as Nash looked me over. He'd stared me down plenty of times in the past, but this was different. Now it was like he was seeing me with new eyes. Whatever he saw, he must not have minded too much, because he broke into a laugh. "Anytime, bro."

Relieved, I turned to Twig. "You were totally right in your video. I've been too caught up in all this Achieve-O-Meter crap. I mean, now I've seen where that kind of thinking got Meticulous. Oh, and thanks for kicking that jerk where it counts, by the way."

She smiled. Not the full-fledged smile she used to give me, but it was better than nothing. For now, it was enough. "Just don't go talking in a British accent and we'll be okay."

"What did you do to Meticulous anyway, Average?" asked Motor.

So I told them.

When I finished, Hollywood was practically drooling with excitement. "Gee willikers! You trapped Meticulous on a dinosaur world? That's doggone cold, if you'll excuse my language!"

Resist scoffed just like Meticulous had on the elevator. "There were cave dwellers. That means the dinosaurs were long gone."

"Not necessarily," said Hollywood. "Maybe the dinos never died off there, and they lived together with humans.

Maybe Meticulous is riding a *Stegosaurus* alongside Caveman Me right now!"

"You think Meticulous will be okay for real?" asked Twig. "I mean, how will he survive on his own?"

Resist shrugged. "He's probably picked up a whole mess of survival skills from Eagle Scout Me."

"Yeah, I figure it'll do him some good to live screen-free for a while," I said.

"But what if this Caveman Me and the others try to kill him?" asked Nash.

"You know Meticulous," said Motor. "He's probably already got them worshipping him like a god or something."

Nash and Twig looked like they didn't buy this theory, but to me it sounded entirely too believable. "We don't have to worry about Meticulous surviving," I said. "We just have to worry about him coming back."

Resist gave the elevator a swift kick. "Then we have to turn this crate off and never use it again."

"After it takes us home, right?" said Hollywood.

"How?" said Motor. "We don't have the right origami codes for our worlds. It's—"

Resist cut him off. "Don't say it's hopeless!"

"I'll get you all home," I said. "Not just you, but these sellouts too." I waved to the trussed-up Mes, who glared back at me over their gags.

"We also have to return all the Mes at Me Con," said Resist. "Including the Missing Mes, of course."

"You mean there's more of . . . you out there?" Twig's face went pale.

"Long story," I said. "I'm sure I can re-create the folds that will get everybody home, but it'll take time." A new wave of exhaustion washed over my wet, cold, and creaky body. "And I may need a nap first."

Hollywood started to panic. "What if the night watch finds us in the meantime? And for that matter, how do we occupy ourselves while we wait? This place doesn't even have holo-TV!"

"Get a grip!" said Resist, though she looked pretty eager to leave too.

Twig spotted something in the elevator car and stepped inside to pick it up. She came out holding Meticulous's MePad. "This was his, right? Would it help?"

"Yes!" Motor grabbed some of the wires from the busted keypad and got to work. In moments, he connected the MePad to the origami drive. "All the origami patterns for the Earths and their portals are still in this thing's memory! Watch!" He spoke into the MePad's mic. "Earth Eleven."

The green octopus in the origami drive twisted and turned as if folded by an invisible hand. The next second it took the shape of a Lesser Antillean iguana.

"See?" said Motor.

Beaming, Resist slugged Motor on the shoulder. He winced but smiled back.

"What Resist means is that you're brilliant and can do anything once you forget about being insecure," I said.

Hollywood nudged Troll so hard the Me almost fell over. "That's what I call hacking, eh?"

Troll scowled at him from behind his gag.

"Funny that Meticulous didn't think of rigging up his MePad to the controls like this," said Resist.

I shivered in my wet clothes, cursing the janitors for leaving the air-conditioning on full blast. "He's smart, but he has tunnel vision. It probably didn't occur to him."

"Or maybe he wanted to take you along for the ride," said Hollywood.

"Why would he want to do that?" I said.

Motor shrugged. "Being an evil genius must get lonely sometimes."

"That's more psychoanalyzing about Meticulous than even I care to do." I said it like a joke, but no one laughed. We'd all realized at more or less the same time that this was goodbye. Nash and Twig must have sensed it too, because they slipped into the lobby to give us a moment alone.

Or maybe they just found all of this too weird.

We dragged the virals into the sea-stinky elevator, making sure they hit a bump or two on the way. After we lined them up along the walls, my friends stepped inside. I stood across from them at the door, none of us knowing what to say.

Hollywood finally broke the ice, tears welling up in his eyes—genuine ones this time. "I've never had any real friends until you guys!" he said, hugging me and then Motor.

I thought I might get weepy too, until Hollywood added, "Thank you for helping me on my actor's journey!"

The rest of us fake-coughed to cover our laughs.

Hollywood moved on to Resist for a hug, but she patted him on both cheeks instead. That cracked everybody up.

"I can't say any of you have helped me on my 'actor's journey,'" said Resist. "But it was pretty satisfying to stop Meticulous together. You Mes are all right."

Motor looked thoughtful before speaking. "You know, I don't think I'll get another mobility cart when I get back. After all this running around, it would feel too . . . cushy." He grinned. "But I will stock up on Diarrhea Delights. I mean, those things come in handy in any reality."

At the mention of the dreaded candy, Hollywood made a sour face. But before he could gripe about allergies, I cut him off. "Guys and gals, I don't know how to thank you."

"Then don't!" said Resist. "This is getting sappy. We know how you feel anyway. We're all Mes, right?"

Motor fiddled with the MePad. "The car should return here when we're done taking everybody home. When it gets back, turn it off. That's the only way to make sure Meticulous won't get hold of it again."

I nodded. "But you know, maybe I could turn it on from time to time and pay you all a visit?"

"I don't know," said Motor. "Awfully risky."

"What's the harm?" said Hollywood. "Come to Earth Thirty-Four! I can show you every episode of *Baker's Dozen*!"

"Pass!" said Resist.

"I wasn't just thinking about a social call," I said. "The first world Meticulous took me to was totally flooded from climate change. I kind of wonder if there's something we could do to help it. And maybe help other Earths too."

"Definitely!" said Hollywood. "It's just like what Resist was telling everybody at Me Con: we Mes could actually accomplish something if we worked together! Especially us four!"

"This is the part where I'm supposed to say, 'I doubt I'm up to the task,'" said Motor, smiling. "But I'll save that for a later date."

"We do make an okay team, sort of." Resist shrugged. "Sure, sign me up, I guess."

I almost started bawling like Hollywood right then and there, but I kept myself together. "It's settled, then. I'll check in soon."

As the doors closed, Motor waved goodbye, and Hollywood gave me an overblown bow. But it was Resist who got in the last word: "See you later, All of Me."

Then the elevator carried them away, leaving me alone in the room with nobody but myself for company.

The MeMinder chose that moment to pipe up yet again. "You have been sedentary for more than five minutes." It started listing the many things I was supposed to be doing at the moment, with no mention of all the stuff I'd already done.

But I didn't let it finish.

I hit the Reset button instead.

Acknowledgments

I'd like to thank the family of raccoons that terrorize me every morning on my predawn jog. The way they appear in the dark, staring me down with their beady eyes and forcing me to turn around and shuffle in the other direction, really gets my adrenaline going and jump-starts my brain. I thought up many of the scenes in this book after some raccoon or group of raccoons scared the crap out of me in this way, so they're kind of like my muses.

Otherwise, I owe undying gratitude to many other lifeforms across the multiverse:

Agent extraordinaire John Rudolph

Editor supreme Diane Landolf

My very thoughtful sensitivity readers, Cris Beam, Tavi Tragus, and Sharane Wang

Erin, Wilson, and Oliver (plus the cats and the bearded dragon)

Mom and Dad, Julie, Debbie, Clay, Skye, Kaley, Ken, Maggie, Willow, Steve, Pam, Eric, and Anna

All the great folks at Random House Children's Books

Kim at Paradigm

Matthew, Mike, Spike, and Yoni, plus Mr. Mullins and Mr. Myers

And a special shout-out to the people who invented the assorted brands of allergy nasal spray I used to ward off Austin allergens while under deadline